WHEN TWO WOMEN DIE

WHEN TWO WOMEN DIE

by

Patricia Goodwin

An Historical Novella of Marblehead, Telling of Two
Murders Which Happened There, 301 Years Apart

Plum Press
Marblehead, MA

When Two Women Die
Copyright © 2011 by Patricia Goodwin

Library of Congress, *When Two Women Die* registered © 2011 by Patricia Goodwin

Cover Design: Christina Goodwin

ISBN   978-0-615-58724-0

WHEN TWO WOMEN DIE

To Marblehead,
in her truest form,
and to all those who love her,
past, present and to come

Acknowledgements

First, I must thank my husband, Tim Goodwin and my daughter, Christina. Tim loves to call me a "natural writer", which kept me encouraged, in the true sense of the word, full of courage. Christina kept the dream of this book alive by supporting me every inch of the way and by providing much needed critical advice, graphic design, and videography (see YouTube and patriciagoodwin.com for *When Two Women Die* book trailers). Because mainstream publishing turned me down flat over and over (thank you, Kindle for making the dream a reality), I was on my own with only Tim and Christina, and a few others, to support me. Those few: Joan Perry, my closest friend for over 40 years, listened - I think - raptly to every historic detail. Tim Whiting, master rigger on the Half Moon, historic replica of Henry Hudson's 17th Century ship, provided me with nautical references. Poets and musicians, Angela Masciale, Dan Zampino, Lee Eric Freedman, Tyrone Hawkins, John Boehmer, Pamela Kuras, Maryl Wilcox and Oen Kennedy who believed in me and in my work.

Marblehead, herself, has been my greatest inspiration. Colonial times had long been a passion of mine before I came to Marblehead. Seeing the place for the first time, with its simple fishermen's houses looking out to sea, and graceful old streets and gardens, and meeting the people here who love all those things too, only fueled that passion.

Marblehead never ceases to speak to me; she is my constant companion throughout the bright days and dark nights, with crashing waves or sailing boats, long trails of moonlight or crystals of sparkling sunlight on her waters, with her bells ringing the hour, her seagulls arching through the sky, and ever-present layers of history, layers of truth, layers of love.

WHEN TWO WOMEN DIE

Preface

For a long time, I have been concerned, and quite horrified, by how we, as a society, perhaps as humans, allow our best and brightest to become our victims.

Almost every day we hear of some promising, beautiful child or young woman, sometimes, a young man, who has been slain. Usually by a career criminal who has not only murdered before, but is still alive, often free, to murder again. These men are pirates.

In 1991, when I first heard about the death of Martha Conant Brailsford[*], who went sailing with her neighbor only to be murdered by him, something happened to me. I immediately thought of another woman, a mysterious Englishwoman, who had died, 301 years earlier, very close to the same spot. Marblehead legend says her screams can still be heard.

Both women, I instantly felt, had died at the hands of pirates.

While I did not want to write a non-fiction account of what had happened, the idea of a fictional book that somehow told the legends of two women, past and modern, who were killed by pirates, began to haunt me.

It was the 1993 murder of Polly Klaas, a young girl who was stolen from her home, raped and murdered by a career criminal, that changed me forever. No one could hope

---

[*]*Martha Conant Brailsford was the descendant of Roger Conant, who founded Salem, Massachusetts in 1626.*

for a more lovely and graceful child, yet this wonderful child was brutally murdered. The circumstances of Polly's death were so horrifying, including the fact that she lay alive but unconscious next to the policemen who helped her murderer when his car got stuck in a ditch; the fact that her abductor was so high he didn't even know which of the girls at the sleepover was Polly, the little girl he had followed home; the idea that Polly herself willingly went with him to save her friends, her mother, and little sister – all the nightmarish circumstances of the little girl's death have stayed with me. This book might easily have been based on Polly.

Maybe, in a way, it is about Polly, and all those like her, vital, beautiful, optimistic, caring people who were taken from us by pirates.

We have made some great improvements, with Amber Alert and web watch organizations, but we still have so far to go. New pirates are appearing every day. Human trafficking, for instance, has become more lucrative than drug dealing. It's terrible, but we have to teach our children: our girls to be cautious to the point of being mistrustful of everyone, and particularly, to educate our boys to truly respect women.

We must heed the warning in *When Two Women Die* from Marblehead's 1690 psychic Ol' Dimond, referring to pirates, "After me, none can help thee. No longer do they stay on the sea."

WHEN TWO WOMEN DIE

"After me, none can help thee.
No longer do they stay on the sea."

- Edward Dimond, Psychic
Marblehead, 1690

WHEN TWO WOMEN DIE

Marblehead, 1690

Chapter 1

Elizabeth Treadwell woke to the darkness and soft silence of early morn. The tender shape of her infant pressed against her bosom fitted perfectly along her neckline. The little head tickled her chin with its feathery down of hair, which appeared almost white and ghostly in the dimness. She nestled Emilie's airy cheek with her own. The child's breath, transient as a flutterby's wing, caught in Elizabeth's eyelashes and entered her nostrils. The smell, thought Elizabeth, was cleaner than anything on earth.

She loved waking thusly, to the stillness of the first hours. However, already she could see the light growing in strength, sifting into the grey atmosphere of the tiny room.

A muffled noise below told her that her eldest girl, Molly, was up and moving about. Surely, though only eight-years-old, she was a treasure to her. The hearth would be burning well by the time she dressed, which she did now, sitting up quickly and tossing her skirt and bodice over her head. She gathered her fair hair into a knot and pinned it neatly. She laced her bodice over her nightshift, then bent to pull on her kersey stockings and stuff her feet into her shoes; she found these where she'd placed them, neatly at the foot of her pallet the night before, thinking while she dressed, how fortunate she was to have Molly's extra two hands working industriously in the kitchen, 'twas like being in two places at once. Instinctively, she hoped that wasn't a wicked thought, for it seemed somewhat devilish to desire the impossible.

The infant stirred and philosophical thoughts disappeared from Elizabeth's mind. She picked up the babe whose wide blue eyes, so like her own, blinked and closed again, only to open and look directly at her mother.

"Pa," Emilie said.

Elizabeth's heart leapt. It sounded almost like a word. The very word she would so like her husband, Tom, to hear. If only he were beside her now!

"Tom," she spoke almost silently, barely moving her lips, but holding the 'm' tightly for dearness. "Tom."

She stroked his bare back with her fingers, so lightly she knew he'd not wake. His strong back, which took in all her fears.

"My love," she said, and her fingers fell and she was asleep.

'Twas a dream she'd had of him the very night before, yet something she'd done a thousand times in her life. So real it had been, she almost felt she could reach out and touch him now - if she turned, perhaps he would be there. Tears sprang into her eyes. No, she mustn't do that. Weeping in the morn only brought exhaustion to her. She gazed at the small sea chest barely visible against the wall, remembering how Tom had taken the larger of the two, for it was to be a long fishing trip out to the Banks this time.

"Eh, eh," Emilie began to fuss, smacking her tiny lips.

Elizabeth loosened her bodice and brought the child to her breast, which Emilie found with sudden energy and satisfaction. Elizabeth forced herself to sit calmly for a moment, for the child's sake. Her own mother had taught her to be at peace while she nursed. But, it was no good. Elizabeth was impatient. She got to her feet, turned and made up the pallet with one hand, clutching the gulping Em to her as she did. She draped a kerchief round her neck so that it hung loosely over the baby's head, and hurried to the next room to wake the other children.

They were already stirring. All except her eldest, nine-year-old Tom, his straw-colored hair stuck up in all directions across the pillow. One adolescent foot was thrust through a hole in the old fustian blanket. Five-year-old Peter sat up in his bed; he was a smaller, angelically fair version of his brother.

"Mother," Peter whispered, groggily, "Tom's got 'is head a' bed."

Elizabeth laughed. 'Twas something she'd often said to Peter; it did him good to catch his older brother.

"Aye, that he does. Cum, lad, get up." She urged Tom, gently pulling his foot.

Tom groaned and turned away from her.

3

Instantly, Elizabeth's maternal alarm sounded. She shook him harder.

"Cum, I need thee! What's amiss, lad?"

He turned and rubbed his eyes; he blinked up at her. His usually bright blue eyes were red-rimmed and buried in dark hollows.

"What've ye been about, Tom?" Elizabeth instinctively feared, running through her mind a list of possible trouble a boy could get himself into in the middle of the night. "Have ye been tiddlin'?"

"Noo," Tom moaned into his pillowbear.

Elizabeth leaned to sniff his breath. The baby drooled on to Tom's neck and he leaped from bed. All at once, the other children, from their beds, Peter and Jane, who was three, burst into laughter, and the tension was broken.

Elizabeth thought she'd caught the pungent after-reek of stale alcohol. There were plenty down by the waterfront who'd ply an innocent with rum just for the joke of seeing them stagger or lose their speech.

Molly entered the little room by the open trap door in the corner and took over the task of fastening Jane into her clothes, which Elizabeth had begun with one hand.

"Does she have to cum in 'ere while a man is gettin' dressed?" Tom complained, pulling his worn linsey-woolsey breeches up over his nightshirt, stuffing the shirt in with an angry hand.

4

Molly rolled her eyes. Elizabeth and she shared a giggle. Molly finished lacing Jane's dress and gave her an encouraging pat on the shoulder. Then, Molly, her petticoats caught up, back and front, led Jane and Peter down the ladder to the kitchen for their breakfast. She eased herself first, cupping her hands out from time to time, ready to catch their tiny buttocks should they slip. Together the three proceeded remarkably quick and agile, Elizabeth admired, down the rungs.

Elizabeth turned to kiss Tom's cheek. The boy blushed and quickly kissed her back.

"Your sister is a comfort to me, as are you when you are industrious."

Tom nodded, reflectively.

"Now, will ye go an' tend the garden fer me, loosen the earth roun' those tender plants n' give 'em room ta grow."

"I'm not a farmer, Mother."

A sudden anger took Elizabeth's breath.

"Do I hear Ned Low talkin' now? Or Tom Treadwell?"

Tom was silent.

Rosie Low, Ned's mother had been Elizabeth's best friend since they'd played at their mothers' feet, and now, they had twelve of their own children playing about them. They'd been pregnant together four times and Rosie was large with child again, but if her best friend's son were leading Tom astray, she'd have none of it.

"I'll not speak ill of my neighbors, but, Tom, ye're my son and a good child. There's many in this town who'll not get up from their sloth to tend a garden, who send to Boston for ev'ry bit of meat an' ev'ry scrap of linen. I'm not one of 'em. Now, you'll obey yer mother an' you'll be learnin' sumthin' useful that mayhap could save yer life sumday."

Tom's mouth hung open at his usually quiet mother's outburst. He nodded and mumbled an apology.

"Nay, thy good work will be sorries enough."

In the kitchen, Elizabeth put Emilie down in the well-worn oak box her husband Tom had made for the children to play in whilst they were little.

Molly stuffed thick slices of cheese into bread, then, stuffed these small meals into the even smaller hands of her brother and sister, reaching eagerly to her. To her eldest brother she handed the last of the venison pasties from the deer her father had killed when last he was home; 'twas a dish usually saved for a man and Tom knew it. He gave his sister a kind smile then before hurrying out on his way. Elizabeth was glad.

She noticed Moll had kept the fire burning hard for the sake of the oven though the day promised to be warm. Elizabeth opened the kitchen door to find the air ominously still and grey with a heavy brume boiling off the hill behind her house. Not a good day for baking, as the bread would not rise easily, fighting the mist as it did. Still, it had to be done. You couldn't wait for a dry day in a wet land, and, besides, she told herself, tomorrow would hold its own task.

Late the night before, Elizabeth had filled the oven with dried maple sticks. These were now embers, which she scraped out, ignoring the blast of scorching air that flushed her forehead and cheeks.

"Too hot," she judged. But by the time Rosie came, her housewifely wisdom told her, the oven would be just right for the kneaded loaves she and Rosie would place inside.

Quickly and carefully, she swept the charred embers with a small broom and shovel and saved them in the ash barrel in the corner to be used in soap-making, an autumn chore she dreaded and would do soon enough, a good deal hotter than baking though it was done out-of-doors. She closed the oven door, thinking the while, mayhap she would steal some ashes out to bleach that new head rail she was working on for Em, or mayhap she should simply dip the cap into the ocean and place it in the summer sun, once done.

Elizabeth heard the first twitter of a bird. She and Molly exchanged a look.

"In a minute, t'will be deafn'n, Moll. Ye best get down there, if there's to be any raspberries t'all today."

Molly nodded, bending to take the little ones' hands.

"Take two baskets and the milk pail. On the way back, stop at the Pritchards' an' see if there's any milk to spare."

Elizabeth's family shared the cow, 'Cilly with the Pritchards; though it wasn't her day to milk her, Elizabeth hoped for a cup or two, which she'd owe, but dearly she wished she had some for Jane and Peter today, mayhap a sip for herself. She wondered if that meant she was with child; almost at any time, she could be. Nay, she be nursin', after all, she told herself, still...

Molly had blushed at the simple mention of the Pritchards. She was hoping, Elizabeth realized, to catch a glance of young Daniel Pritchard, and be glanced at, in turn, no doubt. Such a thing might be frowned upon in what Rosie laughingly called the "dreaded drearies" of Salem, just four miles away, but in Marblehead it was accepted as healthy and good.

She watched with affection as her fair daughter took the milk pail in hand and the two little ones, their tow heads together, readied to follow her out the door like ducklings trailing a mother duck.

"My, my", thought Elizabeth. "How love does continue on in its way."

"I'll stop those birds frum gobblin' up our beer-ries, Mother, I'll git 'em fur ye w'me spee-er!" Peter mouthed through his bread. "If I've anythin' t'say 'bout it!" he added, miming his father's expression, "If I've anything to say about it," causing a lurch in Elizabeth's heart. She smoothed his fine hair out of his still sleepy eyes.

"Ye're not to be spearin' anything, ye hear? John Indian should know better than to give such a toy to a child."

Though he'd been wise enough to cut a blunt edge to the tip in Peter's case, Elizabeth admitted, he had given the older boys, Ned and Tom, real weapons and, though John Indian had taught them all his skill, which was considerable, it gave her a fearsome shudder, nonetheless, to think on it.

T'were near fourteen year ago, her dearest Rosie's own mother had been one of the goodwives to walk out of meeting during the horrors of King Philip's War and, seeing two Indian prisoners being led through the square, had, in a rage, set upon them and killed the heathens with their bare hands. It were none of John Indian's doin', but even Elizabeth's steady heart could not place blame upon Rosie's mother, as her husband had been one of those who'd been shot dead by his trusted Indian neighbor one fine morning, simply by opening his front door.

Now, in more peaceful times, you could see John Indian in happy sport any day, sending his spear clean through the center of the boys' rolling hoops.

Marblehead, 1690
Chapter 2

"Lor' 'ave, mercy, Ned, don' drop iii-it! Oh, thur she go-o! Ye let go yer end, Neddie! Look, she be up-ended, noow!"

Ned's reply was unintelligible.

"What'll ye do when yer cap'n of the *Desire*, un? Up-end she, too? Oooh, never will Lizzie 'low my rise in w' her'n, now t'is sticks n' stones to break thy teeth on!

"Cum, pick up thine end, Ned! Cum, shame on thee, thy muther is w'chil'!"

Elizabeth could hear the clear, deep tones of her best friend's voice coming from far down the path. Well could she picture the drama unfolding just out of her sight. 'Twas not unlike Rosie to drop her sourdough in the dirt. And not unlike Ned to be a reluctant helpmate.

The first rays of brilliant sun sifted through the trees, sending paint into the day, revealing shapes and colors that previously had been hidden in murky shades of grey and blackish green. The moist verdure of maple leaves burst upon Elizabeth's eyes flecked with God's own gold, sunshine, passing through them on the breeze. Lacy ferns unfolded next to ghostly white birch trunks. Small flowers came to life along the roadside: wood violets, white star flowers and blue forget-me-nots nestled between the rocks, yellow and purple clover in deep beds of soft green moss, sweet williams, pinks and wild primroses. Passed now were the meadows of Indian phlox that had given the moon a rosy blush; the fields of blue scilla she loved, and the clouds of wild rose. Passed also, the early spring bulb tulips and daffy-down-dillies that had bobbed their top-heavy heads, scarlet as cardinals or yellow as finches, planted long ago by those who'd come on the first ships with such treasures sewn into their pockets. These first flowers of early spring, so beloved by Elizabeth, and long awaited through the cold winters, had been replaced by summer's crimson columbine, ladies' slippers, pale red bobbles of kiss-me-over-the-garden-gate, bold faced black-eyed Susans, the immortal love-lies-bleeding and bright yellow sunflowers, tall as folk, nodding their heads by the roadside.

Rosie came into sight, disheveled, but undaunted. The staggering abundance of red curls on her head bounced gaily. Her large brown eyes, as always, heavy-lidded and drowsy. In one of her husband's stained and much worn smocks, she looked a mountain of motherhood and good spirits.

Elizabeth laughed to see a bunch of wildflowers waving in her hand.

"Hull-ooo, Lizzie!" Rosie called. "We've come at last! Johnny's just took Joseph, Eli, Nan and Tim down to thy Moll, by the by." She spoke of her five young ones, John, eight;

Joseph, seven; Constance, who was six; Tim, five, the same age as Peter, and Elias, who was three.

Carrying his end of the tub, Ned looked askance or anywhere but straight at her, in his typically disgruntled manner. His sharp features cut a darkly handsome profile into the bright day.

Elizabeth smiled warmly and waved. Rosie carried her baby, Julia, scandalously strapped to her back with a shawl, squaw style. To everything Rosie brought a fresh, childish heart, which Elizabeth admitted, she lacked herself, but dearly appreciated in her friend.

Once inside, Ned let go his hold a little too fast, causing Rosie to cry out as the tub fell harshly out of her grasp. A dull thud was heard as the wooden tub fairly crashed upon the mud floor.

Both women looked at him; he looked straight into their astonished faces with blank eyes. He turned and left the house.

Rosie made an uncomfortable laugh.

Turning her back to Elizabeth, she cried, "Oooh, help me off w'this heavy chil'!" Elizabeth untied the shawl; Julia slid into her arms, a blue-eyed, red-haired poppet, somewhat sticky with drool and the yellow pollen of buttercups.

"These're fur you, my dear." Rosie said, thrusting the flowers into Elizabeth's only pitcher of spring water.

"Ro-sie! What've ye done? Now, I'll have to send Moll to the wellcurb." But, at the same time, with her free hand, Elizabeth, found herself arranging the flowers, blue bellflowers and buttercups, into a more agreeable shape.

"Look at that! Ye got a magic hand, Lizzie Tred'll! I could fiddle w'em all the day an' never get such a pretty posie!"

The two women shared a morning draft of ale and the last of the week's stale bread before beginning their work. They didn't sit long. With both their babies content for the moment in the box in front of the hearth, they busied themselves, standing elbow deep in flour, kneading both their sourdoughs together despite Rosie's grit, chattering as they did, about the children, the weather, their neighbors, for a while content as their infants. Then, after a contemplative silence, during which they deftly folded and patted the kneaded dough round itself into several perfect loaves, Rosie moaned and heaved such a great, mournful sigh that Elizabeth thought she felt her friend's sad breath blow right over her own heart.

"What's to do?" she asked Rosie.

"Naught." Rosie remarked, continuing her work.

"Nay, cum now, tell me. Ye can'na fool me, Rosie. I feel ye sorrows as me own. Tha' sigh came from thy troubled soul."

With that, Elizabeth saw her usually jolly friend plop down on the bench and sinking her face into her floury hands, sob with such abandon Elizabeth was frightened. She threw her arms around Rosie, covering both of them with clouds of flour in the emergency.

"Rosie! What ails thee? Stop thy weeping an' tell me!"

"Ug," Rosie lifted her head, her lips distorted and thick with sobs, "I'm a coward fur even thinkin' on it, but 'twas so *real*!"

"Was it that dream, ag'in?" Elizabeth asked, anxiously.

"Aye!" Rosie sniveled. "'An tha pain, 'ginnin', 'ere." She clutched her enormous belly down low.

Julia began to whimper then, to hear her mother cry so, and Em, also, let out an experimental wail.

"Now, look what I've started!" Rosie joked, coming back to herself. She reached down to tickle Julia's belly. "Hush, hush! There's a dear! Oh, Lizzie, what's to become of me? And my children if Matty wuz to die?"

"He'll not die."

"How do ye know?" Rosie asked, hopefully.

Elizabeth was silent, admitting she did not know.

"T'is bad luck to weep into the bread, I'm sure." Rosie said.

"What has passed, then?"

"It be the same as 'afore, Liz." Rosie cried. "I'm asleep, quiet as love be, an' of a sudden me eyes open an' I see me Matty standin' there, all still an' queer-like, an' Lor' 'ave mercy!" She began to weep anew, she gulped her speech, but continued, "He be holdin' a babe an' it 'pear that gone, dead, Rosie, dead in his arms, an' he d'plead, 'Kiss me, Rosie, dear! Please, kiss me!' Oh, I heard tell of such 'pearances 'afore death! D'ye think me Matty be gone? Oh, Rosie! Wha' 'bout it? Wha' 'bout the *Rosamond*? I fear she be turtled somewheres, tha' I do! An' the pain in me belly, deep and sharp! It bode no good fer the mite! What d' ye divine it do mean, Liz?"

"I dunno. Be he really standin' by thee?"

"Aye, but all thin and froachy, then he do blink out, poof! An' I be more alone than ever I were in all me days w'out him I truly love beside me."

Rosie sobbed anew. Elizabeth sat in silence, thinking of her own loneliness. Her calm was contagious, for Rosie stopped after a while and spoke quietly, "Ye d'know, this chil' be m' eighth, an' bein' 'lone 'as caused me to fret that sorely. Matty didn'a wan' me to bear a'nuther, so fearful were he of it, being more'n seven. He say our luck cunna keep, temptin' fate in sich a way. We fought sorely 'fore he left an' Lizzie, ye d'know how hard it were fer me to see me man go w' cross words 'tween us. I know he be as much to blame as I, but it near broke me 'eart, an' still do."

After a moment of sniffling thoughtfulness, Rosie asked.

"D'ye think I be temptin' fate?"

Elizabeth didn't answer, so deeply did she think upon it. It were common knowledge many women, strong and weak alike, succumbed to childbirth long before their seventh babe. She herself would be at her sixth if she were with child now.

"Do ye think, Lizzie, Ol' Dimond w'd know what the dream d'say?"

"I hear' tell he d'know a great deal 'bout what most folks d'not."

"Mayhap I should go to Ol' Dimond an' ask he."

Edward Dimond was an old man who lived alone at the foot of Burial Hill, where all the ancient folk of Marblehead were laid to rest, there to watch forever over the town and their beloved sea. Ol' Dimond was well known for his ability to gaze into the future or into folks' hearts to find the truth. Once, Elizabeth had heard he'd caused Reuben Treevy to walk all night carrying a log bigger than he was for having stolen firewood from the Widow Moody. Her own Tom swore it were true, having seen Reuben the next day, exhausted and sore to the shoulder with a red swelling he did not remember how he came by. Another time, Ol' Dimond read Ruth Gatchell's very thoughts as she walked by, telling her in her head, but with his own voice, that her mother's pewter porringer had fallen behind the hearth grate and ne'r to fret. The experience of hearing his voice within her, echoing her own mind had knocked Ruth clear off her feet, but find the precious porringer she did, hidden in the ashes.

"Mayhap he kin set yer mind at ease." Elizabeth suggested, thoughtfully.

"I could go this very night." Rosie sniffed, gaining courage from the idea of taking any kind of action.

"Bide w'me, tonight, then," Elizabeth comforted her friend. "I will tend thy little ones."

Marblehead, 1690

Chapter 3

In the blastin' heat of early morn, Ned Low's restless mind was churning as he worked his way up the bothersome hill behind the Tred'll house to where he was sure Tom was, workin' in his mother's garden. He, himself, had just spent the previous hours doin' the same. 'Twas maddenin'. Farmin', milkin' o'cows. An' he stank, too, most o'the time of the milk that spilled on him, every which way, no matter how he pulled. That he might be an awkward milker never occurred to him. The cow, Nancy, was stupid and did not like his touch, he'd told his mother. "Ye be right in yer second claim," his mother had told him.

The breeze brought the smell of salt to him suddenly, a tease of what was soon to be. He couldn't wait. Next year, he'd be ten and would go to sea. He'd have his own vessel, none o' that cuttailin' fer him like Tom'd be at, at his father's side on the *Rosamond*, out of Marblehead. Slittin' the tails o' cod w'children. That w'd be more the like of rottin' in gaol. Whilst the open sea called out. 'Twas the only place fer Ned Low, if truth be told. He longed fer far away places, warm as bed and sweet as honey - Barbados, the Jamaicas, the Spanish Isles. He'd have his own black slaves'n plenty in a jeweled palace on a white beach...

"Hull-oo, jackass!" Ned called to Tom, who was dawdling, resting his chin dreamily upon the hoe. "Le'me shew ye how to quash a weed!"

Ned ripped the hoe out of Tom's gentle grasp. Absentmindedly, Tom had been turning a delicate star pattern round each and every small plant while he daydreamed of nothing in particular.

Ned smashed the blade of the hoe deliberately down on the tender flesh of a young cabbage, breaking it in half.

Tom sucked in his breath. "What've ye done?" He asked, confused and somewhat hurt himself, as if from the blow. He knew t'wd break his mother's heart to see such destruction. If he were to pick the cabbage, to hide the damage, she'd know t'were missin'.

"Mother'll be that sorry, she'll want to know wha' happin' t'it." Tom whined, nervously.

With a quick toss of the hoe, Ned threw some soil over the broken plant, barely covering it.

"Dunna worry ye girlish brow. We'll get 'er sumthin' tasty in its stead."

It being exactly seven in the morning, a family of fat rabbits was contentedly nibbling its way down the woods path that led out of the garden and away from the house. He felt rather than saw them there. If he leaned a bit to the side, he could just discern the furry tips of their ears, never still, flicking in the sunlight.

He'd have to sharpen Tom's spear, no doubt. The man had no concept of how to keep his weapons at the ready.

"Where be thy spear, man?"

Tom looked up, bewildered, still a little dismayed at the loss of his mother's cabbage.

"I dunno. Within."

"Ye should keep it with ye, man."

His own was not by his side, as he'd had to carry that blasted tub, but he scolded Tom nonetheless.

If he'd thought the garden to be heavy with the heat of the sun, Ned was unprepared for the intense heat of the kitchen from his mother's and Goody Tred'll's baking that hit him full force as he entered the house.

"Confound women's folly", he thought, "bakin' on a day that baked on its own."

No one was about.

Almost blindly, in the half-dark, he rummaged through some things on a shelf, Tom's dim-witted sisters' wool cards, niddy-noddies, spindles, to find Tom's whetstone. He opened his deerskin vest and took his knife from its sleeve on his belt; quickly, thrice he slid its blade over the whetstone. He threw the stone back down with a clatter against the wool cards and the girls' other spinning and weaving tools.

He strode outside, lifting Tom's spear from where it rested by the door, as he passed, sharpening its point in quick, expert motions as he walked.

He hated using another's weapon. He had carved his own with his initials, NL, and it were sharper and more ready than this fool's lance. Ah, he would have to make an exception in order to make the kill.

Ned continued on his way as resolutely as any predatory animal. He moved toward the path, soft as light itself, soft as John Indian had shown him.

Not like the rabbit, John had said, like the fox, light as light, straight as his nose to his long, red tail; "Pequawas", make yourself and your spear straight as the fox, straight as the fox.

The spear flew.

Tom turned his head, somnolent and occupied with gardening.

The largest rabbit, the mother, fell. Her belly heaved in short breaths. Terror overcame her soft eyes; terror nearly burst her gentle eyes as she lay on her side, heaving quick breaths of shock.

Her children stopped eating. They twisted their heads, side to side, in confusion.

Abruptly, Ned stepped among them.

Though bare, his heavy foot caused the small ones to jump slightly, as though the forest floor had shaken with the impact of his step.

Tom watched, open-mouthed, unable to say what he felt to his violent friend.

Ned yanked the spear from the mother's body, using his foot to hold her down. Blood splayed over his leg. Without a moment's hesitation, he stabbed the babies, one, two, three, four, collecting their still breathing bodies upon his spear. He neglected to say the prayer of gratitude John Indian had taught him to the young rabbits for the sacrifice of their lives that would feed him. He did not think on it once. Instead, he lifted the spear proudly, dripping with their blood. He laughed at Tom's pallor.

"Ye'll not mind tonight, Tom, when ye're fillin' yer belly w'em. Nay, ye'll not mind, t'all."

Tom knew 'twas true, yet the slaughter had sent shivers through him. Saying as much to Ned Low was useless. Silently, Tom bent his head to his task.

Ned chuckled. Tom was good for a laugh.

Marblehead, 1991

Chapter 4

Cassandra Diamond Hawkes worked hard on her hands and knees scraping the deck of the two-masted yacht, *Heart's Desire*. Though she wore a string bikini, hoping to get the maximum sun exposure while she worked, her skin was as pale as ever, white and pasty, causing a slight revulsion to each crew member who happened to look her way. She thought, in her usual deluded way of thinking, that her figure was decent, which it was, that she fit right in with the other casually dressed workers, which she did not. Her bikini stood out as being too overtly sexy compared to the sun-bleached rags everyone else wore.

She'd gotten a good rhythm going with the scraper stretching, pulling, stretching, pulling. The sun on her back felt reassuring. It was the only nice thing today. She didn't like this boat. To tell the truth, she didn't like any boat since she'd lost her own in her divorce. But, a sculptor couldn't make a living in Marblehead unless her family was wealthy and owned the house she lived in and there were plenty of those. They usually won the Arts Festival too, she thought glumly, as she bore down too hard and took up a sizable chunk of the rich, caramel wood in the mouth of the scraper.

Shit. Quickly, she looked around to see if anyone had caught that, foolishly smoothing the white scar with a spit-dampened finger, which did nothing to camouflage the damage.

Karen stepped over her, agile and light as a cat, with her long, coppery legs in frayed Patagonias.

"Ooo! Nasty!" She cooed.

Typically, Rémi, the foreman, a small wiry man, was over Cassandra's shoulder in a second.

"Vhat! Vhat! Vhat! Vhat are you doo-eeng? Ooh, la, la!" His dry, sun-weathered finger tapped the gouge. "Tsk! Look at that! You'll have to sand that down, Mon Dieu, that's gonna show!"

He stared down at the deck, for a moment, shaking his head condescendingly, "You are such a spaced-out cadet, Cassandra! Sheet!"

"I do know a little something about wood, you know; it is my medium." Cassandra said, leaning back on her heels.

"Yah, yah, yah! I just bet! You so good with wood!" Rémi's voice trailed off in her psyche, though he continued to rant.

You'd think he'd have lost that phony French accent by now, Cassandra thought, he's been in this country nearly fifteen years, but the accent just gets thicker and faker.

She turned away from him and gazed out to sea. It wasn't the serene cluster of yachts she usually saw, white hulls like cups against the sun blue sea.

Cups against the sun blue sea, she repeated to herself, the yachts changed then into yellow, blue and white cups bobbing in the sky above the sea, like a mobile bobbing in an open seaside window...

Her vision was shifting, she was about to go into a reality sleep, something was wrong.

You'd think the absolute, dazzling beauty of the place would be enough to keep anything bad from happening, keep all the pain away, but it wasn't enough, something was terribly wrong, the fishing boat, it was coming in too fast.

"It's too fast," Cassandra said aloud.

"Vhat?" Rémi replied, impatiently squinting his eyes at the horizon. "Oh, my God! He's go-eeng to ram us for Chrissake!"

That stupid accent again, the idea that her Sun God, would ever, could ever ram them, he was her Sun God, her Apollo, hadn't she sculpted him in the blondest wood she could find, just this way, driving his chariot, she gazed with admiration at him piloting in his fishing boat, his white blonde curls filled with salted wind, the way he sailed in summer, bronzed neck and chest, the string of blue beads about his throat, but it was his face clammy with horror, the deep furrow of concern on his high brow that told her everything. She watched with a sense of pride in him, a strong sensation of justice that he should be the one to find her.

"Vhat tha freegin' hell is go-eeng on?" Rémi screamed, waving his arms in frantic circles, "Vhatta you do-eeng!" He hopped from stern to bow and back again as William Cotton slid the fishing boat, at high speed and with only inches to spare, expertly into dock.

Constricting her own lungs and throat, making it suddenly difficult to breath, Cassandra felt the pain only good men and women feel, coming from Cot's heaving chest, the way he ducked his head as Rémi yelled at him and wiped at his forehead with trembling fingertips as though trying to comprehend. In obvious pain, he looked past Rémi at the other men approaching, hurrying toward him from their boats.

It was right he should be the one to find her, wrong that she be tangled in his nets. Wrong, her beauty bloated and decomposed, floating like torn rags, whoever had done this had violated the sea, corrupted the fishing place, he was no sailor, her pretty foot, distorted and tangled, the first thing Cot saw, as he raised his nets, reeling toward him from the water, it told him of the horror, Cassandra felt his heart throb and go sick, rage and go sick again; she felt then the bonds on her wrists and ankles, clumsily tied, tearing at her flesh, the unbearably heavy, dragging weight of the anchor tied to her ankle, why was it there? Why? Something else was tying her down, pulling her down, tied to her wrongly, and the once cool, friendly blue water painfully forcing her nostrils, forcibly entering her ears and eyes, that was not right, the terrible throbbing through sleep in her brain, insisting she wake, insisting, she could no longer feel the warm sun, she knew things, she knew these friendly things, her soul cried out to her in her sleep, wake up, wake up, this is not right!

Marblehead, 1991

Chapter 5

Beth Treadwell, her friend Julie Low Peach and their five children were eating pizza at an upscale Italian restaurant in the mall. Beth's youngest, Emily, was having her pizza indirectly, on her mother's breast.

"Did you ever hear the story about the young fisherman - listen to this," Beth said, reading from what seemed to Julie a very old, very boring book, "who, having returned from his voyage, was walking home and seeing his fiancée standing in the road, handed her a fish from his catch only to watch her disappear before his very eyes."

"*A fish?*" Julie exclaimed, adjusting her shirt, one of her husband Bill's brand new, custom-made, blue linens. "He gave his girlfriend a *fish?*"

"Yes, it's so romantic, isn't it?" Beth teased.

"A fish is not romantic." Julie made a disgusted face as she nibbled on a pizza crust.

"Think about it, though, he caught it, maybe they would have eaten it together."

"Whaddaya mean would have? What happened? How come she disappeared?" Julie said through her mouthful of food. She wiped her greasy hands along her immaculate white shorts and bare legs. "Oh, shit, Consuela's gonna kill me!" Julie grimaced at the grease stains that had trailed her hands.

Beth turned in her seat to see what the children were doing. She glanced around to where the children stood, their noses pressed against the restaurant's long kitchen window, which stretched, floor-to-ceiling, like an horizon along the back wall, where the cooking and the pizza-making process was on display. The children watched in awe: their cheeks reflected the warm glow of the fires that were rising from frying pans and roaring in the brick ovens. Beth watched as a boy dressed in a chef's white jacket solemnly lifted a prepared pizza on a flat wooden shovel and slid it into the open flames in the small brick cave.

"It was called a 'peel' in the sixteen hundreds." Beth said, absentmindedly.

"What was?"

"That wooden shovel, it was called a 'peel'. It still is called a peel. We still use it to make bread, can you imagine?"

"I don't have to imagine. Stop reading those books. And finish your story."

"Stop reading those books and finish my story?" Beth took a sip of iced tea.

"Yeah."

Beth leaned toward her friend with enthusiasm. "The girl had died while he was away at sea."

"Jeez! So, she just faded away before his eyes. What happened to the fish?"

"The fish?" Beth exclaimed, flicking a drop if tea at her friend from the tip of her straw.

Both women laughed. They'd been friends all their lives. A little over thirty years now. They'd played together at their mother's feet and now, their own children played together, not exactly at their feet. Julie was still, what Beth's mom used to call "the instigator", which meant she started trouble. Julie had been the first to take the small balls of pizza dough the waitress traditionally gave the kids to occupy them, flatten a piece into a pancake and throw it, willy-nilly to see where it would land. The flattened dough landed out of sight, but with a loud *splat*. The kids loved it. They began to toss dough and giggled themselves silly. Soon, flattened pieces of dough were flying every which way. Beth, in shock, could only hide her face in her hands while Julie skipped around the restaurant apologizing to businessmen on their lunch hour, and other, more polite, women with kids, collecting the dough only to toss it again.

The middle-aged waitress had remained cool. "Ma'am, I'll have to ask you to stop throwing the dough, please. You're disturbing the other diners."

"Jule, you're bad!" Beth had giggled, near tears.

"Whatever," her friend had replied, tossing another pancake toward the waitress's retreating orthopedic shoes.

Julie was tall and dark; she had olive skin, black hair and mischievous blue eyes. Beth would have sworn under oath that Julie's blue eyes sparkled with mischief. Beth was tiny and light. Julie called her the whitest woman in America. Maybe she was. Her small size seemed only to add to her lightness. Blonde hair, blue eyes, real white bread, she supposed. Peter called them night and day, a feast for the eyes. Julie's husband, Bill said they were the best of both worlds.

Beth checked her watch. Twelve-fifteen, she had to go.

"What're you doin' later?" Julie asked, as Beth leaned to place Emily back in her carrier.

"Got a twelve-thirty meeting with Cassandra Hawkes." She glanced round the restaurant, but didn't see their waitress.

"You've really been working hard on that video, Bethie."

"Well, I think it's important. Don't you?" Beth reached into the pocket of her khaki shorts for her credit card. Tucked neatly into these and a British tan belt, Beth wore a white linen L.L. Bean camp shirt. Her long blonde hair was caught in a tidy ponytail peeking through the back of a baseball cap bearing the sun-faded logo of last year's Marblehead Festival of Arts. "The town should have a visual history as well as a written one. The past is so much a part of our lives."

Julie nodded, "Cassandra is kind of a nut case, though, isn't she?"

Beth shrugged, "Why, because she lost her property in a divorce? Because she's poor and dresses weirdly? I think she'll make an incredible visual statement with her wild red hair - and that voice! Her voice almost sounds otherworldly. She's a direct descendent of both Edward Diamond and Elijah Hawkes, after all. She'll make a great narrator."

Julie looked at her friend. "You still haven't gotten over the fact that you bought her house."

"No." Beth sighed deeply, admitting her friend to be right. Cassandra lived in a rented room, while, she, Beth, lived in Cassandra's ancestral home. It didn't seem right.

By habit, she cast a watchful eye over the kids who were getting antsy again. They'd moved from the kitchen window to the gigantic blackboard the restaurant kept, again, for customer amusement. Julie's seven-year-old, Matthew, in his usual bossy way, was distributing the colored chalk to the others: Julie's three-year-old, Jane, Beth's Peter, six, and her two-year-old, Sarah, who held up their small hands eagerly. "I get blue. Green for Jane. Yellow for Sarah. Peter Rabbit can have pink for his ears." "I don't have pink ears!" "Yel-low for Sar-ah, Yel-low for Sar-ah," her daughter repeated like a song.

Seeing that the children were okay for the moment, Beth's mind wandered along the disturbing line of Cassandra's loss to another injustice.

"I found something horrifying the other day. The Reverend Peter Bours, in the mid-1700's here in Marblehead, accused one of his female slaves of attempted murder. Seems he woke up in the middle of the night to find her standing over him with a knife. He sold her the next day and used the money to commission a portrait of himself to hang in the Church rectory. It's still there. I've seen it, he was a pompous son-of-a-bitch. Bought himself a new suit of clothes to pose in," she read, "dove grey satin breeches, mauve silk waistcoat, white silk brocade neckcloth."

"Cute."

"Yeah, it gets cuter. Seems the slave may have been pregnant with his child. She was twelve-years-old."

"Jesus! Where did you find this? Doesn't seem like anything anyone would write down."

"I know. I found it by cross-referencing diaries and the records of slave sales. 'A pregnant female, twelve years, 87 pounds...' Slaves were sold by the pound."

"Christ-All-Mighty! That really sucks." Disturbed, Julie ran her fingers through her already messed boyish hair.

"I want to do justice to this girl, Jules, I dunno how, but I do."

"In the video?"

"Yes, but I keep seeing a flower garden in her name, you know, down by the Church yard or by the ocean. Or maybe a garden of grasses, always whispering the truth." Beth said, thoughtfully.

"Now, you're getting into poetry. Or would that be the bible?"

"Mythology." Beth answered. "Hey! Here's something else I came across!"

"No more! What're the kids doing?"

Julie turned to see them collaborating on a huge chalk drawing of a sailboat on the sea. Matthew had each little artist intent on his or her own special task, whether \fish under water, rocks, a starfish, or a mermaid.

"Listen, there was a pirate named Ned Low, very infamous, very, very bad! They think he was born in Liverpool in 1690, but they're not sure. Ned followed another guy named George Lowther, the worst pirate ever to sail the seven seas, matey! All that's really known about this Ned Low was that he married a girl in Boston. He was very romantic about love, it seems. Whenever he pressed some poor slob into his crew, he'd ask first if he were married. He'd only capture single men!"

"I'm for that!" Julie laughed.

"His origins are 'shadowy', the books said. Think he came from Marblehead? After all, Marblehead at that time was made up of nothing but fishermen, a few token officials, and pirates, who came and went almost at will. Salem officials couldn't get people here to have a school or a church. If there were trouble, it had to be tried over at Salem court. And, then! No one there could understand our heavy dialect! They probably spoke that way so no one else *could* understand them!"

"Enough, already!"

"He's got your family name, Jules! Could explain a lot!"

"Like what?"

"Oh, like all those detentions in high school." Beth teased.

Julie laughed. "I thought you were gonna say all those Margaritas at Maddie's!"

Suddenly, the two women were surrounded by four proud faces covered with pizza sauce and eight chalky hands of various hues and sizes flying in their direction. Shouts of "Mom! Mom! Look, Mom! Look at our pick-choor!" to which both women responded with "Oh!" and "Beautiful!" Beth picked up Sarah and began wiping her chubby cheeks and hands with a napkin dampened in her water glass. Julie quickly signaled the waitress for the check all the while promising, yes, yes, they were all going to get their ice cream now, right now, yes.

Marblehead, 1991

Chapter 6

When Beth, Julie and the kids drove up, Cassandra was waiting on the stoop of Beth's house, the historic old Diamond house, which Beth and her husband, Peter had bought from Cassandra's ex-husband, Paul Allen, after their settlement. Oh, Beth hated to think of it, but think of it she did, in a flood of mixed feelings and emotions wrenching at her heart every time she saw Cassandra.

"There she is," Julie said sarcastically, unnecessarily under her breath.

It was a sad sight to behold. Cassandra's wild red hair burst from the restraints of the soiled scrunchy she had twisted round it. Her clothes, if you ignored the obvious raggedness, and Beth often thought, Cassandra must have a way of perceiving herself that eliminated the obvious, her clothes seemed of rich fabric, velvets, suedes, silks; though much stained and torn, Beth thought, they seemed often-times as if they had begun life as original Chanels or Diors, and Cass *had* spent much of her early marriage abroad. She sat primly as a librarian: knees together, back straight, hands gently folded. Her brown eyes gazed blankly in front of her, out to sea or inward, Beth could not tell. Sawdust, like sparkling bits of gold, clung to her clothes and hair, and white spirals of wood, like extra blonde curls, dangled from her head and shoulders. Heaped upon her was a deep sadness, a kind of sweet melancholy that Beth couldn't help but feel all unsuccessful artists seemed to hold in their laps.

Julie, Beth and the children broke from the white Jeep Grand Cherokee bright as flags in their crisp, new sports clothes. Beth was instantly and, she knew, unreasonably, ashamed of their show of wealth and good spirits. The kids made a lot of noise laughing and running off to the beach or into the house. Julie called after her, waving over the dark curly head of the child in her arms, "See ya later, alligator! Hi, Cassandra!"

"Hello, Mrs. Peach," Cassandra mumbled, self-consciously.

She's made of pirates, Cassandra thought to herself. What did that mean? She wondered. She didn't always understand the things that came into her head.

"Come on in! Sorry I'm a little late!" Beth sang cheerily to Cassandra, also over the head of a child, this one as light as the sun, in her arms.

"Oh," apologized Cassandra, "I hope this isn't a bad time for you, Mrs. Treadwell."

"I've told you, now, please call me Beth, Cassan - Is Cass okay?"

"Oh, yes, that would be fine. Yes."

Cassandra's speech drifted off as she observed an antique bonnet, framed, on the wall in the sunny entryway.

"A child's head rail," Cassandra said aloud.

"Oh, yes! I believe that is what they were called, very good, Cass! That belonged to one of Pete's ancestors, Emilie Treadwell; she was an infant in 1690! I had it framed on acid free paper. Unfortunately, it's stained, some kind of berry juice, no doubt. I can't believe how fine the stitching is. Look at it! They had such patience back then."

"An' ye'll remember this fine day fore'er, Lizzie Tred'll, by way o'it." Cassandra spoke aloud.

Beth regarded her a moment as the old words fairly crept over her skin. When Cassandra lapsed into dialect, as she often did, it was so vividly real, Beth swore she could feel time shift on the gooseflesh traveling over her skin. Beth swallowed in discomfort.

Now I am in my own house, Cassandra thought. Beth had restored the Old Diamond house to its original state, or what Beth thought was its original state. The hallway's creamy pearl walls were stenciled with ivy and forget-me-nots of federal blue.

Beth smashed her keys down on the antique table by the door. She led the way into the blue and white kitchen, a wide, open space that included the sunny, white dining room that looked out to sea, but Cassandra could not follow.

The house took a deep breath and split down the middle, a wedge of darkness tore down right before Cassandra's astonished eyes, the wedge tore clean through revealing the old room as it used to be, dark, rough hewn, it was a reality sleep, what Cassandra called her reality sleep, more real than what she had to concentrate so hard on, the sidewalks, the curbs, the cars coming, so hard, in order to cross the street, this was more real, this old room and Ol' Dimond walking toward her, smiling familiarly, walking toward her down the dark hallway.

He smiled, sun-worn and wrinkled, his skin as dark as the wet sand left on the beach after the tide had gone out, he smiled gently, but firmly, he told her without speaking as he walked toward her, she read his eyes, kindly, wise, as ever he was in her dreams, "I canna help ye, I canna, no longer do they stay on the sea" and sorrow passed through her along with the cold, familiar form of her ancestor and friend, "dunna go sailing today, dunna," sorrowful and kind, the dank odor of fish, remained, as usual, in her nostrils.

The wedge snapped shut and light filled the house. Sound came back, like a television turned on.

Beth was calling her.

"Cass? Do you want something to drink?"

She was sucking on a popsicle. A blue popsicle from the freezer. The freezer door was open and Beth was busy breaking popsicles in half for the little ones' outstretched hands.

"I don't suppose you'd want one of these," she asked, preoccupied, "I know you only eat natural foods. We have yellow, I guess that's banana, smells like banana, orange, white - whatever that is - want one?" She asked, cheerfully.

"Dunna go sailing today," Cassandra warned, "Dunna."

"Excuse me?" Beth's lips curled blue around the popsicle.

"Dunna," was all Cassandra could remember.

Marblehead, 1690

Chapter 7

Elizabeth and Rosie sat with some of the younger children about them on the sparse grass in front of Elizabeth's cottage. Tim Low and Peter Treadwell made long curving lines of white sea shells upon the green grass while the little ones followed, disturbing the pattern here and there with their fat crawling knees and curious fingers.

The ocean sent nary a breeze their way, the sky being leaden now, and the sea still as darkened glass. But the grass was cooler than the house where baked loaves of bread and raspberry tarts stood in three warm rows along the table. Their work done for the moment, they rested, taking a midday meal of fresh bread broken hot and moist in their hands.

Elizabeth nursed Emilie, her tufted head lightly covered with Elizabeth's kerchief. She and Rosie enjoyed a cool drink of water, fresh from the well that the older children had brought them after their hot morning of baking. To Rosie's amazement, Elizabeth dropped some raspberries in each of their cups.

"What a sweet clarrey that do make, Lizzie! Thy 'and art magical wi' flowers an' berries alike." she said, popping some into her mouth.

"Ah, look, I've gone n'smashed one on Em's new head rail." Elizabeth moaned, looking down at the little cap she was sewing. "Now 'tis blotched fer good."

Elizabeth observed the bright red stain, thinking how bleaching would only turn it purple.

"Aye," Rosie sipped her drink with relish, "An' ye'll remember this fine day fore're, Lizzie Tred'll, by way o'it."

"Mmm." said Elizabeth, thinking on it, musing that such a mark could be a bad sign as well as a good, but not saying as much to her friend.

The crunch of horses' hooves along the sandy oceanfront path silenced the women. Instinctively, Elizabeth pulled her kerchief closer, for the approach of horses meant the coming of someone finer than most thereabouts. Elizabeth worried, too, that neither she nor Rosie were wearing bonnets. Em gurgled uncomfortably.

"She dunna like fine feathers none, neither." Rosie mumbled.

The horses came into view and passed. The Reverend Codger Williams who hailed from Salem, looking stiff and black in new clothes followed by Marblehead's tithing man, Mr. Maverick, in every way smaller and shabbier.

To Elizabeth's astonishment, a shower of raspberries sailed past her nose and plopped against the Reverend's neck cloth. Abruptly, he turned in the saddle, dangerously staggering his horse. Mr. Maverick's steed wavered also, awkwardly to the side of the road. Both riders peered foolishly about them.

The two women looked the picture of maternal innocence, busying themselves with their children upon the grass. Only a few grazing animals and mewing seagulls greeted the Reverend's fierce eye.

The Reverend turned back, unsatisfied. He thought of scolding the women for their brazen, bare heads: one of them with the red hair of the devil; the other, shamelessly shining gold, but he decided not to waste his breath in Marblehead today. Instead, he proceeded on his way with exaggerated dignity. Mr. Maverick followed, aping his superior, but in a manner somewhat pudgier and less dignified.

When the two men were far enough away, Elizabeth whispered harshly, but just a bit conspiratorially. "Rosie! What're ye thinkin'? Never have I seen even ye do such a thing!"

Rosie had that spark she often got in her lazy brown eyes.

"I be that angry, Lizzie, there's no good denyin' it. Mayhap I'll burn in 'ell fer it, but tha' man did tell women over Salem way to wear the black veil to cover their faces in public an' he do fill the young ones w'such terror, tellin' em their pretty faces will send em to eternal damnation, when what could be further frum the truth? My Nan did weep sorely, an she only six year ol', when he tol' 'er tha' 'er red hair was a sign o'tha devil, an' she cunno sleep, when the Reverend know as well as I do such hair harks back to me Gran'pa Hawkes and be no fault o' tha chil's!"

Rosie's lip quivered ever so slightly.

"But, didn't the Reverend John Cotton speak the very next week," Elizabeth offered her friend some consolation, "that the veil would be its own vanity an' that Salem women should be barefaced and proud in the eyes of God?"

"Aye," admitted Rosie.

"The Reverend John Cotton be a good man."

"Aye, that, an' precious rare."

"Amen." Elizabeth said solemnly, and seeing the joke, both women burst into sudden gushes of laughter.

Just then, as if in echo of their mothers' silliness, from the open window above their heads came the slap-slap of bare feet running and the giggling of little girls. A slender young arm appeared and from it, a ball of scarlet yarn flew, making an arch of red yarn over the seated women with their babies. More slapping of feet and a hush.

'Cilly the cow barely turned her head but kept grazing on the common. The Bartoll's pig nudged the red ball with its snout (to the girls' giggling delight) and moved on. The geese, Sarie and Prudence, and their gaggles, fussed and scurried away.

Instinctively, Rosie and Elizabeth turned their heads to see who was coming down the road.

Two boys strolled along, one of them carrying a spear from which seemed to dangle several small carcasses. They didn't notice the yarn until Ned's foot came down upon it and nearly sent him tumbling over.

Close by stood Daniel Pritchard, winding rope round a corner of his father's flaking frame, readying it for the next catch. So intent was he on the repairs for the drying of fish, that, at first, he didn't see the romantic drama unfolding beside him. When he did perceive the girlish prank, Daniel was certain the ball of yarn had been meant to snare him and not that rotten Ned Low.

Rosie's Nan called down from the window, "Ye be caught, Ned Low, on Molly's line!"

"I'll be a fisherman 'fore I'll be a fish!" he cried out, crossly.

"Ho, ho, ho!" laughed his mother, heartily. "A fisherman, not a fish! That's me Neddie!" taking him wrongly, "A fisherman, not a fish!" And, then, suddenly taken ill with her pain, "Oh, Liz, there'd be again, Lor' have mercy on me!" she gasped, holding her belly.

Elizabeth was startled, but did not know what to do. The boys came over to them and Rosie smiled bravely.

"We'll have a bi' o' rabbit this evenin', then." She said with a stiff, greyish face.

Elizabeth thanked the boys, telling them to prepare the bodies for her and take the meat into the kitchen. This they did to a chorus of girlish laughter and commotion inside the house.

"Do ye recall, Rosie," Elizabeth hoped to ease Rosie's distress with a story of their own courtship games, "how we dropped hobnails together that night and no sooner had the nails gone under the boilin' fat than Tom Treadwell and Matty Low came through the door with presents of their best catch?"

"How could I ferget?" whispered Rosie, miserably, seeing in her mind's eye, Tom as a light-haired, fresh-faced boy and her own Matty beside him, as he should be, dark and mischievous, both of them happy, eager as pups, coming through the kitchen door of her mother's house.

"Do ye think, Liz, this babe be dead inside o'me?"

Tears welled in Rosie's eyes, blinding her as she searched Elizabeth's face for the truth she desperately wished would appear there.

"Or do ye think I be already punished fur throwin' stuff at a man o' God?" she smiled, weakly.

Elizabeth reached her hand to hold Rosie's. She took their four hands then and laid them flat palmed on Rosie's belly as if to hold the baby within; both women held their breath together.

Only the warmth of Rosie's silent flesh met their touch stretched tightly in a mound, still and secretive as the sea.

Marblehead, 1991

Chapter 8

Beth loved new mornings.

Earlier, that same day as her lunch with Julie, she had stepped out the French doors into the yard. Her house nestled Burial Hill where all the ancient Marbleheaders were laid to rest and, according to tradition, kept watch over the harbor, where fishing boats and yachts alike also took their rest. The sky was a race of brilliant, white clouds across a pale blue field. The water, which never failed to surprise her with its colors, was a startling aqua, and a mysterious midnight blue or purple in the deeper hollows. Agitated little waves lapped the dock and the small boats with murky tongues.

The men were busy, tying up, unloading. But, not too busy to wave to her. She'd known most of them since Mrs. Z's kindergarten. She waved back, feeling the sunlight on her hand: the day was going to be warm. She sipped the first sip of morning coffee from the mug she held, taking in a mouthful of fresh salt air along with the rich, wakening liquid. Ah, that would be the best sip of the day, she thought. Before the kids woke up, even before the dogs wanted -

She felt the tongues slurp at her bare thigh, nudging her sleep shirt aside, taking up her limp hand, pushing at it till

Beth returned the pressure and patted the dogs' heads and snouts.

"Okay, Tiger, Pizza, okay. I get the message."

Two dogs did a wriggling dance at her feet. Both had been strays, both of dubious parentage. Tiger was mottled, grey and white, medium size and resembled a dirty lapso. Peter liked to say someone's expensive dog got out. That was funny. He always kidded her about her strays. Pizza was part Irish setter. "Which part?" Peter asked nearly every day. Pizza had been playing on the beach one day. Since Beth, Julie and the kids got there early and stayed all day, Pizza had played all morning and afternoon with the kids and had been the only one left on the beach when they were ready to leave, ready to get pizza. Hence, the name. She'd simply jumped into the Jeep. Tiger had just shown up in the neighborhood, started knocking on people's back doors. Literally, with a scratchy paw. Beth fed him once. End of story.

Peter appeared at the door, his dark blonde hair, unevenly bleached by the sun, ruffled with sleep, his favorite Larson mug, slightly erased with wear, clutched in his hand. He was already dressed, if you could call it that, she thought affectionately, in old cut-offs and a faded blue work shirt, that Beth mused, set off his cobalt eyes and sun-kissed skin to perfection. "He's so cool," she thought, smiling at him.

"Hi," he said, sleepily.

She kissed his rough cheek, still warm and creased from their bed. She loved him in the morning. She loved him in the afternoon, she thought, giggling a little, and in the...

"Wha?"

"I love you," she said, kissing him again.

"Mm, me too." His voice echoed into his cup as he took a sip of coffee.

Their friends on the dock cheered and hooted in approval. Peter saluted them with his mug.

Tiger whined and did a dance of impatience.

"Oh, I'd better throw on a pair of shorts and take the dogs out for a run. Can you get Em when she wakes up?"

"I think I can handle that. Don't forget the scooper bags."

"How could I?" Beth called out as she trotted into the house.

Peter yawned contentedly, watching her pretty shape fairly skip into the house. The two dogs barked and jumped in excitement after her.

Beth's neighbor, Frank Girelli was coming out of his condo with his dachshund. He waved, enthusiastically.

"Hi, Frank! Walkin' down the harbor?"

He grinned, broadly. His smile friendly, his white teeth vivid against his dark skin. He got darker and darker every day, Beth thought. Everyone did, including herself, if you could call her biscuit color a tan, but somehow, Frank got darker and stayed darker than anyone. Almost as if he didn't go to work. Peter didn't get dark like that, he got toasted, a sweet mellow brown that just got sweeter and mellower.

She had to admit, Frank unnerved her just a little every morning with his smile. Maybe it was the black moustache. His Italian darkness seemed a little dangerous. Was she prejudiced? He looked more Arab than Italian. Whatever that meant.

He was telling her about his wife. How sick she was. Funny how people looked healthy but weren't. All the trips back and forth to the hospital. How draining it was on their relationship, their life together, how hard it was to keep their hopes up. Beth's forehead knotted in a perplexed frown. She saw Susan get into her Saab nearly every morning. She seemed so energetic and business-like; sometimes, if she saw Beth in the window or the yard, she waved a cheery hello, how-are-you? Not like a sick person at all.

"But, enough about all that depressing stuff. How are *you*?" He grabbed her neck playfully, she could feel his entire hand grip her the back of neck under her ponytail and yank it a little side to side.

"Oh, that's not depressing, Frank." She shook off his hand by bending to adjust the dog's leashes. "I hope you'll always feel you can talk to me."

It was true. Beth had been lending her ear to Frank for a long time now. Peter called him one of her strays. They'd been neighbors for about a year. There'd been troubles at his work, cases he hadn't wanted to take on, but his partners had. She and Peter had helped him pick out his boat. A 28-foot Cal. He seemed incapable of really considering his options, always saying, "You guys decide, you're the experts!" No amount of insisting, "But, it's going to be *your* boat!" could persuade him. When he'd seen the Cal, though, he seemed to know right away. Pete told her later, he was sure Frank was under the mistaken impression it was a large boat, he kept saying so, and Pete hadn't had the heart to set him straight.

"I saw you windsurfing the other day! You looked so - *like a beautiful white bird in your white bathing suit, he thought, I wanted to pluck you from the sea. In fact, he'd squinted his eyes and reached forefinger and thumb out for her and done just that, pluck! She was in his hand! He held her there, tightly, like King Kong had held his ladylove* - so free! You just fly over that ocean, don't you! You own the sea, baby!"

Beth laughed. He really was nice.

"Yeah, I love to windsurf, swim, whatever. I grew up on the water, you know."

He smiled.

"I'll be coming home a little early today, who could work on a day like this? I'm thinkin' of takin' the *Rosebud* out.

Wanna come? You haven't been on her since the virgin sail! I wanna show off all I've learned since then."

"I don't know," Beth hesitated. "I have an appointment. It could take a while."

"Cancel it!"

"Oh, I couldn't do that."

She was frowning again. He hated it when she frowned; she looked ugly.

"Think maybe Pete won't like it?"

"Of course not!"

What a thing to say! Everyone went sailing with everyone else. It was perfectly normal. They were neighbors! Frank was a *lawyer*, for goodness sake.

"Why don't you ask him? Ask him if you can go."

He was laughing at her. His dark eyes squinted against the sunlight.

"Oh, I'm sure it's okay." Beth urged, with a curious, private discomfort. Maybe, she rationalized, she'd take the video camera and get some harbor shots.

They agreed on a time. Three o'clock.

Marblehead, 1991

Chapter 9

The Beach Café was packed shoulder to shoulder that morning, as it usually was on a beautiful day. Almost every stool at the long oak counters was filled, but the friendly clientele didn't seem to mind. They stood amicably with their coffee cups and bagels in their hands or spilled in happy groups on to the benches and even, the curb, outside.

"So, ya think you'll pass muster, Bobby?" Jo called out, referring to the up-coming Muster, the antique fire truck competition the town hosted every year. It was Bob Simmons' baby, so to speak. He planned it, organized it, sweated over every detail, and headed the team that won it, nearly every year. "Firemen" from neighboring towns competed, pumping the handtubs, or old-fashioned fire-fighting equipment, to see which apparatus could spray its stream the farthest.

Bob grinned, approvingly. He was a paunchy man of forty-nine who still had an eye for a beauty. And he could swear Joanna Pritchard, since her divorce three years ago, just got prettier and prettier every time he saw her. She must have settled a great deal. He admired the shape of her legs in tight, black cigarette pants, swinging casually against the wooden stool as she talked to him. Her black hair framed her face in shiny wings that pointed every so slightly to her knockout blue eyes. Absentmindedly, it seemed, she toyed with these points with perfectly manicured fingertips. He'd watched her park her red Cabriolet with one self-assured swing of one of those fingertips on the steering wheel. Fingers laden with diamonds the size of grapes and gold bracelets that jingled and her teeth that flashed white against her deep tan as she tipped her chin for a good laugh.

"Freedom agrees with you, Jo! You gonna come see me whip their asses?"

"Wouldn't miss it!" She winked.

God damn, an' I'm still payin' alimony, he thought, carrying away his decaf.

Jo leaned toward her girlfriend, Carol, sitting beside her at the café's oak counter. Carol's head of frosted, blonde curls nearly covered her face as she drank her Mochachino. Jo whispered discreetly into the soft, pink flesh of her friend's ear into which was nestled a tiny, tasteful pearl, "Just a big pissing contest, if you ask me."

Carol choked slightly on her coffee, and nodded, laughing.

"Guys are definitely in love with their dicks." Carol agreed.

"Oh? And you girls aren't in love with them?"

Mike O'Neill said from the cream and sugar station where he held his Javazooma under the creamer and pumped a few squirts into the tall cup as he spoke which sent Jo and Carol into suppressed giggles.

"Jeez! You're bad!" Mike scolded, teasingly, leaning to kiss the top of Jo's shiny head. "It's too early in the morning for you two. I'm outta here."

Jo looked after him, noting his unusual bicycling pants.

"You know," she remarked to Carol, "most men wouldn't feel comfortable walking around in pink spandex."

Once more, Carol choked with laughter.

Cassandra Hawkes came in, her mass of red hair visible first, her confused face following.

Carol said to Jo, "Beth Treadwell is making a video with her."

"Bethie? No kidding! Oh, I think I heard about it, some historical thing."

"Yeah, you know Beth."

"Yeah, she's into that stuff." Jo said, eying Cassandra's torn and shapeless clothes. "Cassandra has an interesting voice. She'll be good, if she can remember her lines."

"Sam, could I possibly bother you for half a latté?" Cassandra asked the proprietor apologetically. He was a round, little man, who balanced his baldness with a long, grey handlebar moustache.

"Sure, why not, Mama." He exclaimed amiably.

Sam Frost had made a science of, and a small fortune on, recipes for coffee, muffins and pastries. He never minded special requests from customers and they reciprocated by making plenty. Of course, they thanked him plenty, too, with their business. Cassie Hawkes, or Mama Cass, as Sam liked to call her, was an old favorite of his. Together, they'd spent many a winter afternoon in the empty café, discussing life and love and whatever. She was one of the few people who took an interest in his pet peeve, the many wires that crisscrossed the town and destroyed the serene beauty of the quaint old buildings and graceful streets. She had a way, she told him, of looking out and mentally erasing them, but *that* was a talent he didn't share.

Cassandra took her latté cup, slightly more than half filled, over to the only empty stool in the café, next to Jo Pritchard. Her left arm brushed Jo's sleeve and as it did, Cassandra saw a penis, large and comical, right in front of her face.

She breathed quickly to keep from screaming out in astonishment. It couldn't really be there, in front of her, on the counter, she told herself. They'd probably been talking about penises. She glanced over at Jo's neat black cap of hair and Carol's soft blonde curls. She was going to say hello, but they were doing their best to ignore her. She was used to that. Well, she should be, she admitted to herself, sipping the sweet, uplifting punch of coffee, but she never did quite get used to it, if truth be told.

"Want to walk down to the Warwick tonight? 'What About Bob?' looks funny, or did you want to catch the tear-jerker, 'Dying Young'?"

Jo couldn't be talking to her, thought Cassandra. Even as Carol replied, "Sure, let's eat at Marley's and walk over," Cassandra amused herself by answering Jo's invitation in her mind, "Oh, I'd *love* to stroll down to the Warwick with you tonight! Can I be your best friend, *too?*" How nice to walk down to a movie after a leisurely dinner with a friend. She and Paul used to do that. Or they'd skip the movie and walk down to the harbor with a blanket, a bottle of wine and a couple of glasses. The yachts were beautiful, coming in at night, lighted stem to stern, or with an intimate light in the cabin. They'd guess who they were: the newsman, Walter Cronkite; the rock star, David Bowie; and the entrepreneur, Richard Branson, to name a few who'd been spotted there, or sometimes, they couldn't have cared less. They just looked: at the beautiful green walkway that flooded over the water's surface from Marblehead Light; at the gathering black and grey clouds; at the distant, silent houses on the Neck; at each other. She could still see Paul close to her: his dark eyes heavily lashed, his full lips tense with passion, his long hair that fell upon her face.

"I've seen that sad one, but if you want, I'll see it again. What're you in the mood -"

Jo stopped mid-sentence and blanched weirdly under her tan. Her smile disappeared. The corners of her painted, perfectly shaped mouth turned down and she suddenly looked all of her forty-four years. She turned her face away from the front door where she had been scanning the clientele and buried it in her chest.

"What? What?" Carol asked, pivoting on her stool to look for herself, "Oh, God! Let's get out of here!" she whispered hurriedly.

"Morning, ladies!" Frank Girelli greeted them cheerfully, sauntering over to Jo and Carol, making a point of standing close by their stools, trapping them where they sat, in the crowded café.

Cassandra looked up as he spoke to see who had come in. Instead of seeing the business suit he was wearing, *she saw him standing stark naked, dripping with water. Ocean surrounded him and sails splattered with blood flapped crazily behind his head.*

Again, Cassandra knew this could not be really happening. She said nothing. She was glad of her cup of coffee, which she sipped. She kept her face as blank as possible.

Jo also said nothing.

Neither did Carol.

Both women stared stone faced out the picture window. Getting up from their stools would mean brushing against Girelli's body, which he held at close quarters.

Girelli laughed at the women. He turned and walked to the counter where he loudly ordered a Grandé French Roast to go, turning again and again to chuckle at the back of Jo's head. Sam looked over at them twice, as he made Frank's coffee, checking proprietarily to see if everything was all right.

It was then that Cassandra started to hemorrhage, or so she thought, from her vagina, which, to her horror, began to throb rhythmically with a dry, burning sensation like the tearing of the flesh within and her throat became cramped, uncomfortably, then, alarmingly, she choked, upchucking latté back into her cup, she looked at her lap, expecting to see a pool of blood, but there was nothing.

Jo and Carol glanced at her when she choked, as though in a trance themselves. Frank called them a cheery good-bye.

Cassandra watched as Carol sniffed and wiped her eyes. Jo's white lips trembled ever so slightly.

Marblehead, 1690

Chapter 10

Rosie Low climbed Burial Hill along the jagged footpath seeing her way alternately by her excellent night vision and the flashes of dry lightning that burst upon the sky like a candle sputtering in a draft. The leaden heat of the day had broken before sunset, but the wondrous cool breeze that had washed over her and Lizzie and the children at dinner with the door blessedly open, now threatened to knock her over and send her tumbling down the hill.

She hugged her woolen shawl about her. Her skirts whipped around her legs, confounding her balance, causing her to fall forward and clutch frantically on to the clumps of coarse grass that formed the natural, though slippery, steps she was climbing.

"Lor'," escaped her lips, in a worried prayer. She wondered what she'd gotten herself into. Now she'd come this far, she couldn't quit.

Her feet slid on the slick grass; instinctively, her hands wrapped themselves under her belly as if to support the child within. What if she were to fall on her way tonight and mayhap lose the little one, innocent and blameless, in her very effort to save it? And what about her other children? And Matty? If he lived, mayhap he would marry a'gin. Frightened tears threatened to overwhelm what remained of her strength. At the top of the hill, amongst the cluster of graves huddled together there as if for solace against the storms, she stopped to catch her breath.

Her mother's words came to her, so familiar, they'd become her own daily thought, "A mother is more'n one person," she d'say so often, "Yer sev'ral at once, that much be sartin." "An me Rosie be sixes and sevens," her Matty liked to add on.

Instead of worrying her the more, her mother's saying and Matty's voice seemed to renew her.

Well, she didn't know what would become of her or any one of her'n, she could only continue on her way. At the very least, Rosie thought, it isn't raining yet.

No sooner had the thought come, than a terrible bolt of lightning cracked the horizon from heaven to earth and the black sky opened up. Instantly, Rosie was soaked through to her skin; the rain drove straight down as though to pin her to the ground. She was going downhill now; her feet slid this way and that, taking her breathlessly straight down the muddy path almost comically to Edward Dimond's door.

He was within. Rosie could see his betty lamp making an oily halo of light in the center of the window.

To be heard above the wind now crashing about her, Rosie banged her fist upon the old man's door and called his name out desperately, "Ol' Dimon'! Ol' Dimon'! 'Tis Rosie

Low cum to ask yer help!" From so deep inside did she shout, Rosie thought she felt the child jolt with each cry.

From under her pounding fist, the door creaked open.

Through streams of rain, Rosie looked into the vacant stare of Edward Dimond's pale blue eyes.

"Come in, woman!" He said but did not seem to see her, though he looked right into her face. He was a thin old man, bent to his age, with the seeming air of always listening.

Rosie slipped inside. The house was warm and close, reeking so of fifty years of old fish and stale tobacco, Rosie almost choked and wished for the wild wind again. But she soon got used to the stifling air.

"What ails thee this terrible night?" Ol' Dimond asked her, latching the door with such slow, deliberate action, Rosie felt he seemed to walk asleep.

Was Dimond too feeble to be of help to her? She'd not seen him these few months and didn't know if he might be gone too far along in age.

"Speak, woman! Set thyself by the fire, and tell Ol' Dimon' what ye be wantin'."

Rosie crouched on a three-legged stool and shivered in her wet clothes. Water made a puddle round her feet, chilling her to her innards, but it was a relief to be scolded by the old man; it set her mind a bit to rest that he sounded more in control. But where did his inner eye look? So far away did he gaze, it near put terror in her heart. Did he look upon Matty's fate and that of her unborn child?

"I been 'avin' dreams, of me Matty 'way a' the Banks these few weeks, he do 'pear holdin' a babe I b'leeve to be dead so still an' blue it be as the harbor when frozen in winter."

Now that Rosie had begun, her tale caught the fire of her fear and she rambled, "so real like, Ol' Dimon', an' at the same time, all crimmy n' see through. Oh, I fear fer his life, ol' man, an' tha' o' the poor chil'! He didn'a wan' me to bear un, after all, it bein' me eighth. Wha' sh'll becum o' us, me an' th'other child'n if he were to die? An' the pain!" She could feel it now, faint and far away like, deep within, as though lying in wait for her.

"Thy pain be thy fear." He said, simply.

He was not looking at her. He looked instead at the wall, ancient and crude as though weathered from within. Rosie saw nothing there but the rough-hewn shell of some ship lost long ago on these shores. What be he lookin' at? She asked herself as panic seized her. If Dimon' couldn't help her, then where was there help for her?

Dimond reached his hand up then, and Rosie thought he might speak, but he was silent and took down a leather cloak from its hook. This he threw over his head. Rosie watched in amazement as he reached again, this time for his lantern, which he lighted as though in a trance from the flame of the small betty lamp.

He was going out! Leaving her in her misery!

Rosie grabbed at the old man's arm.

"Tell me! Tell me if we shall live or die!"

Calmly, Dimond shook off her grasp. He reached into the dark recesses of the room and pulled out, as though from nowhere, his ancient telescope. Rosie'd heard tell it'd crossed many an ocean on many a vessel, and that Ol' Dimond used it to see the future. Would he see her future through its charmed lens?

Still, he ignored her and his crabby old hand reached, once more, for the door latch!

She grabbed for his cloak but its leather folds slid from her grasp. As they did, hope also seemed to slide from her hold, and she thought, in despair, she'd come for nothing. Mayhap the crazy old man had already left this natural world.

But, then, Edward Dimond half-turned to her, and in a voice suddenly strange and hoarse, he declared, "Thou art well. Get thee home, woman."

Instead of feeling the relief she sought, Rosie was alarmed. There was more, she was sure of it. Why was he going out on such a night?

"Where be thy going, Ol' Dimon'?" she asked.

"There be trouble..." his voice drifted off.

Trouble? Where? Who was in trouble, which one of her neighbors? She thought of Lizzie and the children at home. She thought of the men, away at the Banks. She'd heard tell this weird old man could see that far - was *that* why he'd taken the telescope? To see as far as the Banks? Were the men caught also in this same hurricane, away to the North?

Rosie's heart thumped fearfully, and, she thought, with a sinking spirit, "The dream be true, then," but she felt along with it, another insistent, powerful beating within her, the heart of her unborn.

Dimond opened the door. The huge gale greeted them. Rosie threw up her hands against the sand and debris that whipped across her face.

Then, as though he'd somehow mastered a godly strength, his old frame suddenly stood stalwart while spirals of wind raged about him; Ol' Dimond turned to her and hollered something she only thought she heard, so mingled was his voice with that of the storm.

"After me, none can help thee!"

And he was gone. Of its own accord, the door slammed shut behind him.

Rosie stared helplessly at the closed door. The silence of being so suddenly alone seemed to roar in her ears, louder than the storm that slashed torrents of rain upon the rattling windows and pounded the tired old walls. Then, as though to encourage her on in what she knew she should not do, the baby inside her, whom a moment ago she'd feared might be dead, gave a hard kick to her belly and Rosie stood up and followed Ol' Dimond out.

Marblehead, 1690

Chapter 11

The old man moved quickly, incredibly agile for his advanced years. He seemed to move forward blindly, on the faith of his third eye, while Rosie struggled in her awkwardness and could not keep up. She climbed and slid backward on the wet grass, alternating between excitement and frustration. Finally, she had to allow Ol' Dimond to go on without her.

She found him easily enough at the summit, there amongst the graves, in dark silhouette, a craggy, old shape with his cape filled with wind, blowing wildly about him, and his straggly grey hair standing on end, catching the eerie, flashing light. Old Dimond peered into the night sky through his timeworn telescope. Only God and he knew what he saw there, thought Rosie, as she stood exposed to the stabbing wind and rain.

He looked to the Northeast, toward the Grand Banks, where Matty and Tom and most of the town's other fishermen were right this minute. What did he see? Rosie wondered, what was happening to their ships out there, for Marblehead usually sent out as many as possible to fish the Banks, four or five ships together might be caught in this storm.

Suddenly, Rosie heard a strange, booming voice nearly as loud as the thunder coming from the small old man and filling her ears, "Men of the *Rosamond*! All hands! Hear me now! All hands! Hear me, Edward Dimon'! I be thy helmsman and thy captain now!"

Without thinking, she fell to her knees and crouched behind a gravestone, hiding herself, for the voice was not of this world, that she d'know, and she trembled there, listening now without wishing to listen, wishing she were at Lizzie's or at home in her own bed or anywhere but soaked and shivering behind a stone in a graveyard while Ol' Dimond's madness overtook the very storm that threatened to blow them both off the face of the earth.

More than five hundred miles to the northeast, the *Rosamond* labored heavily upon cold and churning seas, floundering, having swallowed rain and ocean alike till she gasped for breath like a man near drowned.

Matt Low held fast to the very pin rail he'd tied earlier that morning in a stillness that had crept over his skin like a chill warning of what might come. He did not think of that now, except as a ghost of a thought, that hovered somewhere behind what was happening. He thought of nothing now, but holding on to the rail and the line that stretched taut from it, frantically gripping with his fingernails the slippery rope that chaffed the skin of his quickly numbing fingers and let him know he was still alive.

How the *Rosamond* had gotten to this sad condition, he did not fathom, only that she pitched and reeled so that her deck cried out; she moaned and creaked an eerie, suffering lament.

Instinctively, he sought his captain, who was nowhere to be seen nor was the helmsman, and when he strained his neck, to forecastle or stern, helmsman, captain, gone as dead men.

The tiller slammed helplessly from side to side, as an arm broken.

Perhaps he should try to reach it.

Even as the thought came to him, both his feet were lifted from the deck and tipped over his head and he was swept round by a sudden rush of water; he gulped water and spit out into water. The salt taste of the sea, often so compelling and thrilling, what used to fill his nostrils with joy and swell his heart with anticipation, now overwhelmed him. He did not know he was a rag doll, he thought, now I am a rag doll in God's hands. Was it really God's hands that thrust him about so? And what had he done to deserve such treatment? Terror overcame him of his Lord who could pick him up and toss him aside like a child's toy. But, still, he hung on for his life and would not give in, even to God.

Some time later, he was sure he heard the ship's bell ring, long and far off as a phantom bell. But, the clapper was secured, this he knew; he'd witnessed it himself, by chance, as he'd passed by earlier, that same earlier... It rang again, angrily, frantically, urgently. No, it rang like a broken thing, without a message, except that it was not right, not right.

He held on. Am I going as mad as the sea? He asked himself as he turned his eyes skyward. Water streamed over his face and poured down upon him from the black sky. Where were the stars? The clouds, the moon? All means of measure, all means of assurance, gone from the vacant sky. The *Rosamond's* bow flung itself up and down like a rocking horse, nodding, he imagined, in his fright, answering him, yes, yes, yes. This is real.

Shreds of line, broken loose, whipped his aching arms, as he held tight. Once, in a flash of lightning, he was sure he saw Tom Treadwell slide past him like a sack of grain. Blindly, he'd reached a hand out for him and gripped a flailing shroud, a shredded sail.

Tom's descent was broken by the cracked base of the windlass. He crashed against the fractured wood that saved his life, but gave him the scar across his cheek he was to bear from that day onward.

They were long past trying to save the ship. Now, a heavy sleep visited Matt Low, a deep lethargy threatened to overcome his numb and bleeding arms. Desperately, he wanted to let go.

The wind screamed in his ears, occasionally, a word flew past him, reverberating in the hollows of his ears, that must have come from one of his mates, "Please, God!" or "Dam'me!" He heard, once, "Doomed!"

He wanted to let go, only the constant reminder of what lay about him, in wait, the dark void of the sea. Like a freezing man, he warned himself not to sleep, though it were sleep he wanted more than anything.

His head fell backward as if separating from his neck, then, he thought he had passed out, for the screams of the wind and the men drove so loud, they reached a pitch he could not hear and entered into an ominous silence, like a thick brume of silence upon the sea; the *Rosamond* and all upon her, seemed to float in timelessness and a welcome serenity.

'Twas then he heard, or thought he heard, another voice, peculiar, but clear and distinct, "Men of the *Rosamond*! All hands! Hear me now! All hands! Hear me, Edward Dimond! I be thy helmsman and thy captain now!"

So commanding was the voice, so familiar, he recognized it instantly as a voice from his home, though he were so far from home and in so much trouble. The recognition brought new spirit and energy to his exhausted limbs, "Aye, aye, Cap'n Dimon'!" Matt heard himself cry out, surprising himself with his own strong voice somehow tunneling through the dense silence.

"Rig a sea anchor! Get her head to the wind!" He heard the voice command, and the response, fine and brave, 'twas the voice of his friend, Tom Treadwell, "Aye, Cap'n!"

Matt watched in wonder as Tom actually stood, and with another man, made his way to the forecastle. Once there, their arms lifted as in a strange dance illuminated by flashes of lightning that froze the men in weird, electric silhouettes as they unlashed the lines that held a small boat and heaved her over the bow. Empty, she sailed the black sky between heaven and the sea, into the ship's churning slice. She hit and filled with foaming water, creating a good drag. A fine sea anchor streamed to weather, her line stretched taut, she balanced the *Rosamond* well, till she could hold her chin steady and proud.

"Clear the pump well!" Ed Dimond seemed to whisper directly in Matt's ear, as though it were a secret meant for him alone. He responded instantly and with fervor, "Aye!"

He let go the rail he'd held for dear life and found himself suddenly flat on his belly, crawling along the deck, now a river he tread upstream, to the hatch.

Once there, he rode the stream face-first down the ladder, his hands out before him, and as he landed, he felt the clump of sail that had worked its way round the bilge, choking it.

"Clear the well!" commanded the whispering voice in his ear once again, and Matt Low's hands began twisting and turning the shredded canvas. His head above water, he breathed deep, plunged under, worked the piece of sail this way and that till it ripped the more and broke free and the stream flowed over him more quickly and with direction.

"Man the pump!" he heard from the deck, and soon, came the regular thumping and churning, like the voice of a fellow doing his job alongside him; the pump was working.

It was not long before the *Rosamond* righted herself and the eerie voice of Dimond bade the crew farewell. A wounded Tom Treadwell took the helm and a weary Matt Low sank to the deck below, his limp arm flung over a rolling hogshead of salt pork, marveling at the straightforward motion he could feel about him, rocking every knowledgeable inch of his body, telling him the *Rosamond* was sailing now and true.

The wind still beat about him, but Ol' Dimon' stood steady, his arms held broad and high as though in prayer.

Through the rain about her eyes like tears, Rosie saw him suddenly collapse from exhaustion. His shoulders sank and his old head fell forward to his chest. A great, deep sigh came from him then, and she knew whatever he had been doing out there, he was done.

As he turned and began to make his way down the hill, he passed so closely to her hiding place that Rosie could've reached out and touched his bony hand.

But, it was the old man who startled her when he took hold of her trembling shoulder with his formidable, wizardly grip.

"Get thee home, woman. Thy husband an' all aboard have been saved, but thy trials be not over yet."

With that, Rosie caught her breath like a chastised child. Instantly, she jumped up and hurried back to Lizzie. She could not wait to tell her friend what had transpired.

Marblehead, 1991

Chapter 12

Awkwardly, Beth held the cue cards for Cassandra to read. The camera stood steady on a tripod to Beth's left, keeping her well out of view.

Cassandra squinted. Beth turned to see if the sun was in her eyes. She thought she'd figured that out. Maybe the sun had moved; they'd been there so long now.

"Every road, every house had what were called *flakes*, ("Whew," thought Beth, "finally, she's rolling.") the racks where the fish were dried before being sent to market. The best of the catch, called the *merchantable,* were shipped off to Catholic Europe; the *middling*, or secondary quality fish were kept and eaten at home; the *refuse*, or worst fish, were shipped to the West Indies or Jamaica.

The smell was atrocious. You couldn't walk down the road without - "

Cassandra stopped.

Beth let the cards fall to the ground in exasperation.

"That was good, Cass, why'd you stop?"

"Someone's waving at me," Cassandra squinted, looking down the street, "I don't know who he is."

He was naked this morning, she wanted to say. *Soaking wet.*

Beth sighed. She turned to look.

There was Frank, outside his condo, waving in mock cheerfulness, as if to say, "Remember me?"

"Oh, my God, I forgot! I'm supposed to go sailing! Is it three already?" She looked at her watch. Three-fifteen. She was late.

"Wow. Have we been doing this for almost *three hours*?"

They hadn't gotten very far. This was going to take forever, Beth thought as she gathered the cards together. They were awkward, because she'd had to make them large. They kept slipping from her grip, sliding to the ground.

"Dunna." Cassandra muttered.

Beth couldn't understand her.

"What?" Beth waved back to Frank Girelli's eager form. She held up one finger to indicate that she'd be just a minute.

"Don't go sailing today."

"I have to, I promised. Oh, God, he's waiting for me."

Beth piled the cue cards hastily whacking them together, which caused them to slide. She'd have to come back for the camera. No one would steal it, she reassured herself, this was Marblehead. No time to take it off the tripod now, no footage of the harbor, she guessed. Oh, well, she'd have to edit out any modern anachronisms, anyway.

"I can take them for you," Cassandra offered, meaning the cards.

"No. I have 'em." She stuffed the cards under one arm. They hit the ground and trailed noisily. Cassandra followed close at Beth's heels like a bridesmaid desperately trying to catch the train.

"It's okay, Cassandra. Pete!" She called to her husband who was busy in his workshop. "Pete!" She called over the screech of his power saw.

"Yeah!" The saw whined to a halt.

"I gotta go sailing!"

"You *gotta*?" He laughed, lifting his safety goggles.

"Yeah! Can I? I promised Frank. Is it all right? Em's asleep in the carriage; I'll put her down before I go. Sarah and Peter are at Julie's. Half an hour, forty-five minutes, tops! I'll tell him, just around the harbor, okay?" She leaned the cue cards against the shop wall.

"Can I leave these here?"

"No."

"Come on."

"I'm kiddin'. If Em wakes up, I won't be able to hear her, not even with the intercom."

"Well, I can't take her."

Peter regarded her as he wiped his hands on a rag. She seemed kind of short tempered, like she did under stress, when she felt uncomfortable. He was about to say, "Are you sure you want to go?" when Frank appeared suddenly blocking the sunlight filtering into the shop, darkening the room.

"What's the hold up? Something wrong?" He asked. "Can I borrow your wife for a few minutes, Pete?"

Peter squinted at Frank's silhouette. He was tempted strongly to say, "No!" and go back to work. Something about this guy rubbed him the wrong way. But, he figured Beth knew what she was doing by befriending this loser. Besides, she looked so flustered and embarrassed; he didn't want to be the one to embarrass her further.

"Yeah, sure, go ahead. I'll clean up now and go inside."

"I'll just put her down, hon' before I go. She's good for another thirty minutes or so."

Pete nodded, uneasily. He kissed Beth's cheek that she offered him. It was sweet with sweat and a flake of sugar, he thought, from the sugar cookies she'd been munching with the kids earlier. He'd recall, later, that he hadn't been able to give her a decent kiss goodbye, because that monster had been standing there.

"See ya!" Frank called over his shoulder. His broad, dark hand came down and sat, spider like, on Beth's white T-shirt.

As they passed, the sunlight streamed back into the shop. Pete turned on the saw and went back to work. Maybe, he thought, he'd get in a few minutes before he had to check on Em.

Ten minutes later, Cassandra watched the two people walk down the street toward the harbor. Frank's tall, dark body towered over Beth's slight form. Her ponytail bounced. She's always so happy, Cassandra mused. *Then, after a moment, inexplicably, Beth disappeared completely and Frank Girelli seemed to be walking alone. Then, he was walking toward Cassandra, dripping wet again, fully clothed this time and alone.*

As usual, Cassandra was terribly confused.

Marblehead, 1690
Chapter 13

"Lord, help me! Oh, sweet Jesus, Savior! Help me now!"

Elizabeth stirred in her bed. *She was dreaming. She dreamed she stood on the beach and Jesus was walking toward her on the water; he wanted something. He wanted her to do something.*

"Good God, save me! Oh, please! Save me!"

Then Jesus disappeared and the ocean grew tall; it towered over her! It swelled before her where she stood in a great, deafening roar. For a moment the shining, monstrous wave hovered there, twitched and made as if to fall upon her.

Elizabeth sat bolt upright in her bed.

"Jesus! Help me! My savior!"

Immediately, Elizabeth knew it was no dream. It was real. A terrible alarm was being raised - right outside her window in the night.

A woman's horrible cry and worse, the muffling of that cry by a hand across her mouth as she tried to shout. And the laughter of cruel men at her fate. Laughter, and the roar she'd thought was a tidal wave, smashing against the windows, flapping against the glass like flags in a gale, thrashing nails of rain against the house - a full nor'easter raged.

Instinctively, Elizabeth leaped from her bed and made as if to go out and help the poor woman, heedless of the storm. She grabbed for her clothes and then stopped.

Elizabeth looked directly into Peter's stunned face. He was sucking his thumb like he used to when he was a babe. Behind him stood Rosie's young ones, Eli, Nan, and Tim clinging to the older ones, Joseph, Johnny and her Moll, who cradled Jane in her arms.

Elizabeth threw down her clothes and held her arms out to the children; all of them ran to her and buried their terrified faces in her bosom or clung to each other's trembling bodies.

"What does it mean, Mother?" asked Molly.

"I dunno, 'cep' there be...trouble..." and her voice trailed off as she left the children suddenly, and falling to the floor, began to crawl to the window that faced the sea.

The children started a whimper to see a grown-up in such a strange position, crawling on the floor.

Elizabeth turned and put a finger to her lips.

"Hush," she whispered, "Ye must be quiet now if ever in yer lives, more quiet than sleep. Kin ye keep silent?"

Only the older children were able to nod their heads. Elizabeth glanced at Emilie's gentle body fast asleep in the folds of her mother's bed, and Rosie's baby, Julia, curled up beside her. What a contrast their serene profiles made with the shrieks that pierced Elizabeth's brain with their terrible desolation. 'Twas one thing to think on a scream in yer mind, thought Elizabeth as she crawled, and another to hear it actually rise out of the soul of another human being. Elizabeth's heart tore anew with the anguish of each cry. Her back, as she crawled, shuddered.

"My Lord help me, please, what have I done to displease you? Take this suffering from me! Jesus! Jesus! Oh, my Lord!"

It was a lady, Elizabeth realized, by her fine speech, a proper English lady, not a Marbleheader whose coarse burr and clipped manner of speaking was unmistakable. How did she come here?

It hardly mattered, Elizabeth told herself. Here, the poor dear is, more's the pity.

Agonizingly, her heart breaking with every cry, Elizabeth crawled; she reached the window and peered over the sill.

'Twas hard to see through the glass, clouded by rain streaming down, making the surface thicker than fog. But, heavy shapes lumped to and fro in front of her: suddenly an arm jutted out from the huddle, an arm with its hand in the shape of a fist in a downward motion over the middle of this huddle of bodies, and once, what might have been a knife, glistening in the pulsating lights of the storm, followed by the most heart-piercing screech of all and the tormented groans from she who lay upon the sand.

"Why, Lord, why? I've never hurt anyone!"

Again, the triumphant laughter of men.

The woman sobbed, deeply and loud, now, the sobs of a wild animal, guttural, savage, and to Elizabeth's mind, the wind seemed to shriek all the more, in sympathy with her.

"Save me, God!" the woman screamed a vicious command.

Then, Elizabeth saw, beyond the figures, in the sheltered waters of the cove, suddenly illuminated by a flash of lightning, the unmistakable shape of a Spanish galleon, and the black flag that flew upon it. 'Twas something Elizabeth had seen only once before in her life, the dancing skeleton brandishing a sword.

"Pirates!" The word escaped her lips.

Immediately the children let out a squeal and Elizabeth froze, lest the men hear them and turn their violence toward her home, but, luckily, they heard nothing, except the storm and their own fearsome shouts.

Elizabeth crawled back to the children, who were huddled in a shivering mass. Emilie and Julia began to kick and fidget in their sleep.

Elizabeth was struck with a thought. The ladder!

"Dears, I must bring the ladder up! Wait here fer me and be silent!"

With that command, Elizabeth turned and left the children. Sorely, she felt their terror at her back, but she had to pull the ladder up. Oh, the pirates could light the entire house ablaze if they wished, but at least she could do this much.

Elizabeth took hold of the heavy ladder by the handles at top that her husband, Tom had fashioned there for just this purpose. She pulled and the ladder moved but a little.

The boys must have heard her efforts, because at once, Peter, Joseph and Johnny were by her side, heaving the ladder from the side rails and rungs till bit by bit, they had it up, and closed the trap door with a heavy thud and slid the iron latch.

In the dark, mother and boys faced each other in satisfaction for a moment only, then hurried back to the others.

Elizabeth picked up her sleeping baby and held her close, for her own consolation, more than the child's.

"Molly, take Julia! All of you, cum, git into bed," she directed the others. Eagerly, they climbed under the covers, still warm from Elizabeth's body. Elizabeth got in with them, and held her own tightly to her. She pressed her lips to Peter's forehead, then to Jane and Moll. She had ten children about her.

"My dears, we must be silent, for there is nuthin' we kin do."

More than once, Elizabeth's brave spirit caused her to start to leap from her bed and rush out to help the woman. More than once, Elizabeth made to reach for her clothing, throw them on in defiance and fling herself upon the men who had the audacity to hurt another human being right outside her window! But, she could not. It would mean certain death. Not only for herself, but also for her children, and for anyone else who tried to help in the entire town of people: her friends and neighbors, whom she was sure, were listening now, helplessly, in their homes. All would be slaughtered, to no avail, as all the able-bodied men were away at the Banks, and only women and children and a few old men could possibly come to her aid - and be killed in the effort of trying to help.

Tears fell down Elizabeth's cheek. Her own mingled with those of the children, as they clung to each other and listened.

Elizabeth remembered a man, once when she was newly wed and but a girl, a big man, fiercely bearded, clothed in rich rags, high boots, smelling of dark skin and strong, unrecognizable, exotic scents. He'd burst into her kitchen one day, thrown a fistful of strange gold coins upon her table and told her to hide him. In her shock, she'd only stared at him, dumbfounded, and after scurrying about the little house like a caught squirrel, looking for a suitable place to hide, he'd dashed out as quickly as he'd come. English soldiers were seen later that day, their scarlet coats bobbing on the hillside like poppies in the summer breeze.

And Elizabeth thought of her dear Rosie heavy with child, rushing out into the early rumblings of the storm. Though as capable as she was wild, she was out there somewhere, as vulnerable in this storm and trial as anyone.

Her heart beat hard in her chest and perspiration tingled on her upper lip and in the palms of her hands as she clutched the little ones to her. What of her Tom and Rosie's Ned, she thought, who were supposed to be tending the hearth at the Low's? Would they be able to keep to such a domestic duty and be wise enough to stay within if they heard pirates below them in the cove?

Elizabeth doubted the two boys would contain themselves. Her heart ached at each new fear. To think how serene they had been at their evening meal!

They'd shared a fine dinner, the fourteen of them, peaceful and fine as any, the boys standing to give their sisters a place on the bench; Tom and Ned standing on their own at one end of the table.

It seemed unbelievable to her now as she cowered in her own bedroom, that she, Rosie and the children had dined on broiled rabbit, potatoes, wild dandelion, fresh bread and ale, with the rare treat of raspberry tart for dessert, in complete comfort and peace, notwithstanding Rosie's growing anxiety about going to see Ol' Dimond, which seemed a small worry now.

She and Rosie had eaten from the same trencher, as they had when they were little, and the clack of their wooden spoons touching had soothed their loneliness, for she and Tom, Rosie and Matt, would've eaten from the same trenchers as husband and wife, when at home.

The door had stood open to the stirring evening breezes and the gentle beginnings of sunset.

Now -

The woman screeched for nearly an hour and then, more horrible than all their terror combined, Elizabeth thought, came the dreadful and sudden silence that followed the last of her cries.

The men seemed to shuffle off, but Elizabeth's heart pounded wildly to hear another commotion among them, their own frenzied, masculine screams, shouts of "Get 'im!", "Black worm!", "George Lowther!" A name Elizabeth had only heard was the worst, most fearsome pirate of any that ever were.

Then, silence. If the beating storm could be called silent.

Marblehead, 1991

Chapter 14

The sunlight streaming into the doorway was suddenly blocked again. Peter looked up, expecting to see Beth and that guy, what's his name, but it was a dark-haired woman, vaguely familiar in the blindingly bright light, a customer, maybe?

"Can I help you?" Peter asked, turning off his saw again.

Jo just stared at him.

She'd been walking, up on Burial Hill. She was a power-walker and usually set off after her daily "three glasses of vino" lunch to avoid sluggishness; she hated to waste an afternoon drowsy. She'd worked up a good pace when, suddenly, she'd stopped dead in her tracks.

Beth Treadwell was walking to the harbor with Frank Girelli. He had his hand on her shoulder. Jo could feel that hand, heavy and broad, on her own shoulder. It made her shiver, even in the stifling heat of mid-afternoon. Her heart lurched wildly. She watched as they approached Frank's boat, *Rosebud*, a word that sent a pang of disgust through her now. The dogs weren't with them. They were going sailing! She watched in horror, unable to move, until she actually saw Beth's topsider make contact with the *Rosebud's* gunwale.

Beth was on that boat with him!

Without consulting her mind, Jo's body turned and flung itself toward Beth's house. She'd heard Beth's husband worked at home, some woodshop thing: she hoped it was true.

"I'm Jo Pritchard." She began, breathless from her race down the hill.

"I've seen you around town. Is there something I can help you with?" Peter asked, cautiously, alarmed by this agitated stranger in black spandex. He hated spandex; made people look like robots. And this woman couldn't have looked more like a robot if she had a mechanical head. She stared back at him through blue reflective sunglasses; she was strapped around the waist with a beeper and a huge water bottle. Peter hoped she wasn't one of Beth's nutty friends. She sure could bring home some screwballs.

Jo couldn't speak. What, she thought, should she tell him? She was beginning to panic: her therapist told her not to panic. She could feel the sheer panic rising from her gut, the inside of her mouth went all icy, because, suddenly, she realized, she had to tell him, this total stranger. No one knew - except Carol. Even Frank seemed oblivious, like he'd talked himself out of it. She knew what he thought had happened. In his little mind that squirmed like a sick animal.

Her mouth twisted in anguish, "Beth's on that boat with him."

"What?" She had his full attention now, boy. He looked at her face, gone white as a sheet under her tan. Her brow furrowed, she gnawed at the knuckles of her right hand jammed into her mouth. The sunlight filtered round her, floating with sawdust like tiny winged insects settling.

"You can't let her go with him. Do you have a boat?"

"What are you talkin' about? Of course, I have a boat."

Peter's heart slammed hard against his chest.

"What the hell is this? *Who* are you? What the hell are you tryin' to tell me?"

Em's cry broke through the intercom.

"Listen, I gotta get the baby."

Peter turned to go into the house, which was joined to the shop by a covered walkway.

Jo followed him down the quaint brick path Beth had put down under the portico roof, the bricks look really old, Jo noticed in her confusion; little purple flowers grew in the cracks.

"I'll watch her." Jo told him.

"I don't know you."

Jo grabbed his arm.

"You have to go after them. They've probably passed the headland by now."

They regarded each other a moment. Jo tried to tell him with her eyes. God, if he were a woman, it wouldn't take any more than that.

The baby was wailing.

"He's dangerous, do you understand me?" Jo cried desperately to Peter's back, following him into the house, up the stairs, into the decorated nursery.

Peter picked up Emily, who whimpered and nestled gratefully into his embrace.

"Listen," Jo took Peter by the arm again, upsetting the infant slightly, "I went sailing with him once. He raped me. Do you think I like busting into your house like this? Telling you things I've never told - you've got to go after her!"

Peter's first instinct was to tell her off and kick her out. But, something about her eyes, so sincere, so frightened under their heavy black make-up, blue pools floating in tears, frustrated, frantic -

"What! Why didn't you - That's not the kind of thing you should be keeping to yourself!" Peter adjusted Em's arching body in his arms while he reached for the phone.

"It's not the kind of thing you go around telling people." Jo defended herself.

"Well, it should be. Bob? Bob? It's Pete. Can you pick me up on the dock in two minutes? Yeah, two minutes! Yes, in the boat! I don't think I can (already his hands shook so much he could barely hold the baby and the phone at the same time) - it's - (he couldn't bring himself to say, 'Beth') - an emergency! Yeah, yeah, thanks."

Peter hung up. He handed Jo the fidgeting child.

"She just needs to be changed. Diapers in the -" He couldn't think of the words, changing table.

"I got it," said Jo.

Marblehead, 1690

Chapter 15

As Rosie hurried from Burial Hill, the sudden shock of a woman's piercing screech electrified her entire body.

She stood stock still among the graves.

"Lord, help me! Oh, sweet Jesus, Savior! Help me now!"

What was that? Rosie asked herself. A woman, no doubt, in trouble. No one she knew, sumthin' odd. Had she really heard it?

The voice came again.

"Good God, save me! Oh, please! Save me!"

'Twas a lady! A real English lady! How came she to be at Marblehead? Rosie wondered, even as her flesh shivered with each cry. Though she was drenched through, she pulled her soaked shawl about her. She listened, gazing almost blindly into the sky, as the ghostly grey clouds of night hurried past her on the storm.

Rosie pondered on what she'd heard. She knew of every happening in the small settlement and no new ships had arrived to bring such a lady. Mayhap, one'd come that very night to take shelter in this harbor from the storm.

"Jesus! Help me! My savior! Oh, help me!"

Rosie cringed; the voice suffered so. But, who would make trouble upon a lady? No sooner had the question come, so did the answer. All the men of town, good and bad, were away fishing at the Banks. Outsiders must have come.

Pirates.

Now, she could also make out the rough voices of men, were they cheering? Laughing? It was hard to discern with the poor woman's misery and the madness of the hurricane whirling about her. The rumblings of the men followed every scream as thunder follows lightning.

Rosie realized, though Burial Hill was close upon Lizzie's house, she could not allow her shape to be seen running down the street, just a few feet from the men. Surely, they would seize her, too! And she with child! She cradled her belly to her, as often she did, for her own consolation and comfort. Her skin felt warm and alive through the cold fabric of her skirt.

She would have to approach the house from behind.

The trees gave some shelter from the rain, though they leaned frighteningly this way and that in the furious wind, as Rosie made her way to Lizzie's garden path, through the woods, past the Pritchard's uprooted flake, thrown far and pressed against their cottage with the wind that leaned upon it, past the cow shed, while the woman wept and prayed; Rosie came up to Lizzie's in time to see the dark house, still, as though holding its breath, watching -   "Save   me,   God!"

came the worst screech of all, louder and clearer than all the rest, and the men's glad shouts that followed, celebrating her pain.

Tears filled Rosie's eyes as she hid in the woods behind the house; upon the very path she'd traveled so gaily earlier that morn. Listening to this woman's anguish was its own torture, she thought. She wanted to fall down and sob herself. Instead, she peered out from the shelter of a tree trunk; the familiarly rough bark a strange comfort to her cheek. She marked the house seemed secure enough, Lizzie and the children, probably safe inside. The pirates seemed some small distance away, unconcerned that the townspeople in their beds were listening witnesses to their crime.

Indeed, there seemed to be a bizarre, unspoken pact between pirates and the people of Marblehead. If these be pirates, thought Rosie, they'd not bother those that dunna interfere with them. Unlike the upright town of Salem, Marblehead minded its own business. For years, pirates had come and gone almost unheeded by the townspeople, except for the payment of coin and hogsheads of rum, sacks of sugar and bolts of cloth that did conveniently fall into their hands from ships that bore the flag of black and bone.

Then, her heart froze in a panic as she remembered the boys, Ned and Tom, alone at her house. They were supposed to be mindin' the fire. Never would such a homely chore keep them within if they heard the woman's cries!

Without another thought, Rosie turned now and began to run. She did not keep to the path, but changed direction. Rather than take the time to go round the marsh at Oakum Bay, as she and the children had that morning, she plunged into the tall reeds.

Immediately, she was submerged in mud and water up to her knees. Heedless, she dragged her heavy skirts through the mud; laboriously lifting each weighted leg as if in delirious, dreamlike motion. The reeds licked her face with coarse cow tongues as she struggled through the small marsh. She clutched at their bristly stalks for a wavering support.

Once, she startled a family of quails, hidden deep in the grass. Their fat bodies smelling of earth flew directly into her astonished face; frightened wings, fluttering over her eyes, battering her chest, and then, gone.

After a few minutes of toil that had passed like an eternity, Rosie came out of the reeds beside her house, a small linter on the flats.

It seemed quiet.

In the alternating blackness and flickering light of the storm, Rosie could discern no signs of activity. Her instinct was to shout. She wanted to scream for her son, if only to relieve the great pain of fear in her bosom, but the screams of the woman filled her, her very sobs were enough for the sobs of all women and the laughter of the men, for all men. And, the vision of a pirate's face being turned in her direction from the sound of her, Rosie's, voice was too terrifying; the vision rendered her silent.

Rain streamed down her face, or tears, she could not tell.

She ran toward her house, clutching the unborn child to her. She ran and she saw something, something very bad, and heard, too, oh, a bad sign, bad, what was it? The terror filled her now, as she stumbled in the mud and slid, the dry terror in the mouth, open and crying without sound, the terror only a parent can feel.

For, the bad thing was the sharp wind that blasted the kitchen door open and shut like shots from a musket, and the bad sign as Rosie fell breathless against the open door -

the fire had gone out.

"Ned! Ned!" she screeched then, in a scream that rivaled the wind, "Ned!" she shrieked along with the woman, and her voice was mingled with thunder.

Marblehead, 1991

Chapter 16

The sun shone too brightly turning the restive ocean into flashing mirrors of light. They'd caught a fair wind off the causeway and sailed easily out of the harbor. Beth had welcomed the chance to crew, but there hadn't been much to do. The *Rosebud* was easy to handle. Frank had done his part, but seemed to lack concentration. He kept turning her way and grinning idiotically when he should have been minding the helm.

To make matters worse, Beth noticed not only were the halyards poorly coiled, but they'd been cleated with slack in the luff. It drove her crazy. Her expert hands itched to reach over and secure them properly. It seemed a terrible injustice to her, who always tried so hard to do things right, that they were sailing with things done wrong.

"Looks like we're on our way!" Frank exclaimed, smiling down at her from his perch on the rail. "Wanna drink?"

"No, thanks. I'm fine."

He disappeared below. Beth took the opportunity to set taut the luff and coil down properly.

Then, wind and sail reverberated truly in her ears, the sea rustled like silk against the bow. With the sun on her face,

Beth took the helm; she sighed, now, this was nice, she thought, content. Beth was content for a second only, when suddenly, she was sure she heard down in the galley, a wine cork pop.

Her heart caught in her throat. She heard wine glasses tinkling.

Well, so, she told herself, he was an adult; he could have a glass of wine if he wanted. Lots of people drink on board. She and Pete never did, but that didn't mean -

Frank was coming. Why did that sound like a warning?

He sat down next to her. With a sheepish grin, he began pouring two glasses of white wine.

"I really don't like to drink alcohol in the sun." Beth informed him; she hoped nicely, but, firmly.

"Oh, don't worry so much. You won't melt. White is harmless anyway. It's the red you have to be careful of."

"Why's that?" Beth asked, taking the glass she was handed, but not drinking.

"Oh, I dunno," he stretched his long legs. "It just seems like it might be poisonous. Deep and dark, can't see what's in it. You know?" He chuckled into the recesses of his glass.

He was being silly now. She supposed that was a joke, about the red wine. She didn't really believe it, but it was a nice try. She felt sorry for him; he was going through a lot with his wife's illness. She, herself, had had a close friend who'd died of cancer. She'd told Frank the story before, on their many walks. One day, Laura had a stomachache. She went to the doctor and was diagnosed with pancreatic cancer. A few months later she was - gone. Someone she'd seen, someone whose voice she'd heard nearly every day volunteering down at the elementary school. The first time Laura wasn't present at an event had been Family Day in February. The kids had made albums and Beth had stopped to admire Laura's daughter's. She was the first to untie the pink ribbon that held its painted covers closed. The strong resemblance to Laura and her daughter in every face, grandmother, aunt, uncle, cousin, whether in 1940's France or 1960 America had wrenched Beth's heart. She'd walked home and sobbed the whole way, pained by Laura's absence and her presence, agonizingly obvious, at the same moment. Snow had fallen that day, so slowly, drifted really, a snow sun-shower, and the sun had pointed through the trees like the fingers of God.

Beth took a tentative sip. Maybe, she reasoned, if she had a few sips, it would seem like she was drinking and she wouldn't offend him.

"My wife loved sailing. She really misses it. She's too weak now. This was her boat; I bought it for her, really."

Yes, he'd told her that before. Frank repeated himself often. Beth assumed it was comforting to him to retell things about Susan. Still, Susan didn't seem weak.

Beth nodded politely and took another modest sip of wine. She hoped she wouldn't start to feel that horrid, suffocating feeling of getting drunk in the sun. Well, she'd ask for a drink of water if she did.

Frank gazed wistfully at the bow.

"We used to make love right *there*."

Beth stiffened. Twice before he'd launched into inappropriate talk about his and Susan's sex life together. She'd told him right off, she didn't feel comfortable hearing about such private matters. Well, she'd just have to tell him again.

"Frank, I'm sorry Susan isn't well, but you have to stop telling me about things that should be kept private."

"I know, but we're such good friends, I thought I could tell you anything."

"Well, of course, if it's something -"

Then, he brightened. His dark eyes opened wide as if he'd suddenly had a great idea, and to Beth's horror, he giggled so weirdly, it unnerved her.

"Hey," he interrupted her, "Did you ever have an air bath?"

"A what?"

"An air bath! I'm kind of a health nut!"

He stood and yawned extravagantly, spreading his long arms, opening his mouth wide, and so leisurely, that the sudden quick move to rip off his shirt startled Beth.

She sat with her mouth gaping.

"Let's sail au natural." She heard him say, just before he dropped his pants.

Marblehead, 1690

Chapter 17

Tom Treadwell and Ned Low were sleeping side by side, Ned in his own bed, Tom, in the trundle beneath him. The fire they'd been charged to tend flickered peacefully, but low. Unknown to them in their restful slumber, a storm slapped the windows and sent whistling drafts vibrating through the chinks in the walls that had long since lost their pine pitch seal.

In his sleep, Ned wiped his face with the back of his hand, as a particularly stiff wind sent its salty spray across his forehead.

In a sudden, he bolted upright to find Tom standing over him, white as a ghost and shivering madly in his nightshirt.

"Hell's bells, man, whad'ye about?" Ned spoke crossly.

Then, he heard her.

"Lord Jesus, save me! Good Christ, have mercy!" The woman shrieked.

He looked at Tom.

"'Tes a lady." Tom told him in awe, nervously twisting his nightshirt in his thin hands.

"Ye no better'n an ol' woman, Tom Tred'll", Ned complained as he stood and shoved his leather breeches up over his nightshirt and belted them in one swift motion.

The woman cried out again.

Bloodcurdlin', to be sure. He didn't recognize the voice. 'Twas odd, somehow.

He looked up at Tom; gathered his friend's clothes together and thrust them at him.

"Ye look 'bout like those rabbits this morn." Ned remarked with some satisfaction. "Are ye cumin' or not?"

Ned reached for that which he never traveled without these days.

Marblehead, 1991

Chapter 18

"What kind of a fuckin' freakin' asshole fuckin' names his fuckin' boat *Rosebud*? I feel like we're lookin' for a fuckin' sled!"

Peter slammed his fist down on the cockpit dash, causing the compass to rock and bob under the force. Immediately, he jammed the pained knuckles in his mouth.

Bob Simmons, at the wheel, refused to tell him to take it easy. He was pretty shaken himself. And more pissed than he could have imagined. The son-of-a-bitch had raped Jo Pritchard. It stuck in his throat like a thorn.

They'd been out for hours. This was the third time they'd circled the islands off the coast of Marblehead, Salem and Gloucester without spotting the Cal.

"Have ye seen a 28' Cal, the *Rosebud,* outta Marblehead?" Bob had repeated so often, he thought he'd go insane if he heard himself say it once more. All he'd gotten in the way of response had been the typical absent-minded replies, "No, what was the name?" "No, maybe." "We'll keep an eye out." "Out of *where?*" or worse, "Hey, Bobby! How's it goin'? How's fishin'?" and he'd had to cut them off, rudely. But, he couldn't even think of that now, he was so frustrated, sick to his stomach. He didn't know which way to turn. He wished they could fly. Probably wouldn't get a helicopter up unless she was already -

"I'm headin' back," Bob said. "Maybe, they're back."

Peter just looked at him.

"He named her *Rosebud* to attract women."

"Yup."

Bob turned the wheel sharply. Jo had always seemed too bright for him, too rich, too glamorous, too huge. Her smart mouth, well, she made him feel stupid. Now, this new vulnerability. She seemed soft as a flower. The pain inside him was like her pain. He wanted to hold her, to comfort her, holding her in his arms would deaden his pain as well. Then, miserably, he knew, he'd never hold her. Never.

He didn't dare imagine what Pete was going through.

They motored past Children's Island, then Fort Sewall. Slowly, Bob's small lobster boat, *Handtub*, puttered into the harbor. He wove round the bigger yachts, cruisers, catamarans at the mouth of the harbor, further in, round the smaller fishing boats, sailboats, dinghies -

"Jesus Christ! There she is! The fuckin' Rose, fuckin' bud! Fuckin' asshole! Oh, man, thank God! She's back! Bob, man, I can't thank ye enough, man!" Peter slapped Bob on the back, even buried his face momentarily into Bob's thick bear-like shoulder. Bob could feel Pete's teeth on his flesh as if his friend were grimacing or smiling, he couldn't tell which.

But, Bob didn't smile. Seeing the *Rosebud* in her mooring was no comfort to him.

It took Peter another second to catch his mood.

"Fuck! That doesn't mean jack shit, does it?" He moaned.

"Nope."

"Man, my first impulse is to jump on board and beat the living crap outta 'im. I fuckin' wanna take this boat right up Orne Street to see if she's h-ome."

"Take it easy, Pete."

There, he'd said it and it'd done slightly more good than he'd thought. Pete actually took a deep breath and seemed to control himself a bit.

The *Handtub* slid into place beside the *Rosebud*. Peter hopped neatly from one boat to the other.

The stillness caught Peter like a net. The Cal seemed unoccupied. Two towels hung from the boom, dripping on to the deck. Peter didn't know which way to turn. The cabin door was locked. He kicked it violently, over and over, but it didn't budge. He lay on his stomach, pulling himself along the gunwale until he had peered through every porthole: he saw no one. He began rushing about, peering into the water over the sides of the small boat, calling to Beth, at first in a normal tone, but his fear building, he found himself screaming her name, as if the loudness, the urgency of screaming would cause her to materialize. Suddenly, Pete admitted to himself, she wasn't there.

Bob could hear him. Not only the screams, but his feet pounding over the deck of the boat opposite. And, then, Pete leaped back on to the lobster boat, stumbled into the cockpit. He was beside Bob, silent, breathing heavily, his face ashen.

Bob said nothing. He maneuvered the *Handtub* out of dock, in order to bring Pete as close to home as possible. He let him off near the beach at Lovis Cove and watched him wade, his tired limbs still able to push the waves aside like a strong fish; he staggered on to the rough sand, climbed over the sea wall, waited impatiently, visibly heaving with breath, for the traffic. Bob watched, helplessly, as Peter ran down the street like a madman and disappeared rushing toward the house he shared with Beth.

Marblehead, 1690

Chapter 19

Before they were out of the marsh, they saw it.

"'Tes a Spanish galleon," Ned whistled through his teeth in admiration, "If I be a sailor 't'all, I d'know it, an' sure."

Tom noted the flag.

"A jack n' sword."

"Aye," Ned whispered in awe.

The woman hadn't stopped screaming. Not for a moment. Ned did not want her to stop. Her cries filled his black heart with excitement. His fine lip curled in a smile.

"Pirates." he said. "There they be."

They stood in a rough circle laughing, growling down at something in the sand. The whites of their eyes caught the lightning and glowed against their charred skin. A crazed abundance of wiry hair grew from their coarse faces and poked from their kerchiefs and caps. On their belts, gold buckles flashed and the knives held over their heads glinted on their way down.

Some dark hulk covered her on the sand for a time, but it rose from her and she shown like the moon, silvery, white, wet with rain and blood. They heard crying, moaning, laughing, cheering.

Ned forced his way out of the reeds and on to the beach. He felt Tom's birdlike body that had been clinging to him fall in a heap.

He must've swooned, the lily-liver, thought Ned, but Tom hadn't. He'd hidden himself behind a large rock on the sand.

Partly in foolhardy response to Tom's weakness, partly in mindless bravado, or the desire to communicate that he, Ned Low was there! Ned stood then and leaped upon the very rock behind which Tom Treadwell cowered.

He let loose the ancient Indian howl John Indian had taught him, from deep in his bowels it did come, and Ned knew, as he threw the weapon, that the furious nor'easter would send its wind with him, send his spear swiftly to its mark and true!

A large, dark shape let out the squeal of an enormous pig, leaped into the air and fell. Deep within its mark, Ned's weapon stuck up in the air, a dark silhouette in the night.

The woman went on screaming as though nothing had changed, but all the pirates turned at once to see from whence the spear had come.

The tall boy standing upon the rock.

They rushed at him. Several bulky men made the short distance across the beach in seconds. Too late, Ned jumped from his perch.

Violent hands caught his light frame in midair.

His cries mingled with those of the woman, grown fainter, now. His feet flailed wildly upon nothing. His thin fists beat like sparrows' wings against the broad and powerful arms of the men. For the first time in his young life, Ned Low felt unable to help himself. A new and alien sensation overcame him.

He was afraid.

"Wha' 'ave we 'ere? Whose mite ar' thee?" Foul breath of tobacco and India spice blew into Ned's face from black teeth and drooling gums.

"Murderin' 'cuss, 'ee dun in me fren', Jim Quarl'! Let's do 'im likewise, tha 'cur!"

"Ah, he were nuthin' bu' a black worm, tha scurvy'd take 'im! Tha mite's dun 'un a service! Put 'im out, early like! I likes 'im! 'Ee's a malc'tent sprite! How'd ye like ta join our crew, mite, 'n sail tha seas wi' GEORGE LOWTHER!"

A cursed name, Ned recognized, with fear and esteem.

"Eh?"

Struggling to break free, Ned did not reply.

"Ha! Ask ye mutha if ye kin cum!"

With that, Lowther flung Ned down upon the naked woman on the sand.

Ned looked directly into her vacant eyes, caught in the act of pleading with the heavens. He slid upon her white skin, slimy as a long dead fish.

Then, he felt himself lifted again and held aloft by the jeering man.

Anger swelled in the young boy then, and indignation that he be raised and lowered at another's will. He wrestled the air to the delight of the pirates who roared with laughter at his futile efforts.

"Mark, if 'ee don' squirm like a li'l eel on ship's deck!"

Ned twisted his body till he faced George Lowther and, with purpose, spat in the pirate's eye.

"That from Ned Low! Let me down, rot yer guts!"

The pirates stood in utter silence then. For a moment only.

Then, Lowther let out another burst of his putrid breath in a weird, terrible chuckle.

"Ned Low, ye be mine!"

Ned felt himself flung over the man's wide shoulder and carried toward the water's edge. His breath came quick and shallow, his head reeled with sensations. About him as he moved: the pirates' eerie faces, coarser then any he'd ever seen, scarred, pocked, ferocious in expression, the hair of savages, braided with shiny beads, matted with mud, stiff as dung, blackened teeth and open, red mouths, the stink, foreign and overwhelming; the moon swinging crazily as a lantern in a storm; the woman's white body, still as death now; the silhouettes of men shoveling sand over her; and the very last thing he saw, he wasn't sure if it were real, so uncommon strange did it appear, the horror he should feel himself, there, on the white face of Tom Tred'll, bobbing over the rocks like an apparition and for some reason, he couldn't figure, growing smaller and smaller.

Marblehead, 1991

Chapter 20

Peter banged on the door of Frank Girelli's condo. Banged was putting it mildly. Peter took his fist and tried over and over to put it through the door and into Frank's sick, smug face.

"Step aside, Pete or I'll have to do this alone." His friend, Jimmy Martin advised, calmly. That was his job, calm. He'd been a cop in Marblehead for fifteen years. Things were handled calmly here until they had to be handled another way. He and Pete had grown up together, but that didn't help.

Peter was anything but calm.

Girelli opened the door. Pete rushed him, stopped only by Jim's broad chest and the arms that blocked him expertly.

"Where the hell is my wife?" Peter growled desperately through his teeth.

"I'm sorry, do I know you?" Girelli asked, pleasantly.

Pete thought he could kill him right then and there, cop or no cop. But, he was a good man, he reminded himself, not a degenerate. Beth wouldn't want him to strangle the life out of this creep. Beth wouldn't have - he thought he was going to weep. Not in front of Girelli. He braced himself.

"May we come in?" The officer asked.

"Ah, well, I'm kind of busy."

"I'll bet." Peter fumed.

"It'll only take a minute."

"Well, okay. Don't mind the mess." Frank apologized, coyly as he opened the door.

The condo was impeccable. Pearl grey wall-to-wall, navy blue sofa, glass coffee table. Tall windows looked out to the ocean, wide and silent.

Peter got lost for a moment staring out the window at the lie of the serenity he saw there.

The three men stood and faced each other. Girelli didn't invite them to sit.

"Did you go sailing today, Mr. Girelli?" Officer Martin questioned.

"Oh, I've had a busy day, Officer, let me think. Yes, yes, I believe I did go sailing today."

"Were you alone?"

"What's that?"

"Were you alone, Mr. Girelli? We have a witness who saw you in the company of Beth Treadwell. Is that so? Did you go sailing today with Mrs. Treadwell?"

"Why, yes, I believe that is her name."

"Mrs. Treadwell has not returned home, Mr. Girelli. Do you know where she is?"

"She hasn't? Well, no, I have no way of knowing where she is. I left her off on the pier, then I came on home.

Maybe she went on some errands. You know women! Their errands can take forever!"

"You son-of-a-bitch!"

Jim's heavy hand landed firmly on Pete's shoulder.

"When you say 'the pier', you mean, Graves Landing?" he inquired politely.

"Of course! That's where you land, isn't it? So, she hasn't come home, yet?" he added, slyly.

"Do you know where she might be?" The policeman asked Girelli. He could feel Pete's muscles tense under his grip.

"You asked me that before. No, I don't."

"She didn't say where she was going?"

"No."

"Did she greet anyone, stop to talk? Maybe accept a ride from someone down at the landing?"

"No," he hesitated, considering these possibilities. "Nope, not that I saw."

"Nice to be able to go sailing on a workday." The officer sounded friendly. "Did you go to work today?"

"Oh, no, not today. Actually, I haven't worked in some time."

"You haven't?" Officer Martin sounded surprised. "On vacation?"

"No, no. I'm thinking of changing careers." Frank mused.

"Really? Giving up the law? You are - were - a lawyer, is that correct?"

"Yes, I was. But -" Frank sighed deeply, "I could use a change, you know?"

Officer Martin smiled.

"Maybe, you can be a astronaut next," suggested Peter.

"All right, Mr. Girelli. Stay close, we'll talk again."

"Sure thing! Anything I can do to help! I sure hope she pops up!"

Peter, on his way down the front steps, froze. It took all his self-control to keep walking, away from Girelli.

Girelli waited until the two men were almost to the street, before sending his parting shot.

"When you see her, tell her I said 'hi'!" He called out in his most neighborly tone.

Marblehead, 1690

Chapter 21

"I bl'ee 'er silence be 'arder to bear than 'er screams."
Ruth Gatchell spoke in a breathless hush.

Solemnly, her neighbors nodded their heads in agreement.

They stood, with faces as grey as the sickly dawn, on the beach from whence, they were sure, the woman's screams had come. Elizabeth Treadwell was there, so was Rose Low, so also, their neighbors, Ruth Gatchell, Sarah Pritchard, Rosie's Grandfather, the elder, Elijah Hawkes, Miles, his brother, also advanced in years, and several others, shivering with horror as well as the dampness of the early hour, though the day promised to be warm. Already, a fresh breeze stirred in the trees, blowing off broken branches, dead clumps of leaves. It seemed all the town's flowers had been sacrificed the night before; they made clumps of rotten softness about the townspeople's feet, tempering the sharp effect of other debris from the storm, scattered on the beach.

They stood close together in a protective circle. Their serious faces looked down upon a carelessly dug grave in the sand.

"'Tis our duty, then." Eli sighed, "No good denyin'."

With these words, he knelt and pushed the loose sand away from the surface of the grave. In slow, reverent sweeps, almost as though he were preparing her for burial, Eli brushed at the sand until the beautiful, white body of the screeching woman was revealed.

Together, the neighbors gasped and exclaimed at what they saw.

"Oh, mercy!"

"How kin this be?"

"Oh, wha' 'ave they dun?"

Eli shook his old head. The sharp Hawkes features had stayed with him in old age: the elongated nose, and the broad, high forehead. His dry, grey curls, once as tender and vibrantly red as Rosie's, his granddaughter, fell like a curtain of sadness over his noble countenance as he looked down upon her.

"Who would use beauty so ill?" whispered the usually silent Miles Hawkes, from out of nowhere. Unmarried all his life, and facing old age alone, except for the company of his elderly brother in the evenings by the hearth and sharing side-by-side pallets, Miles stood dumbfounded, stunned at the mistreatment of such a beautiful woman.

Her body had been badly beaten. She was purple with bruises, about every part of her white skin, as though purple tried to overcome white as her natural color. Dried, caked blood smeared her so, making it impossible to see her wounds except where the blood was thickest. Her white, slender fingers still gripped the sand that would eventually wash from her hold with the tides. The third finger of her right hand had been roughly sliced off. Her exquisite face wore an expression of utter disbelief. Her eyes still sought heaven.

One of her breasts was near cut away, exposing the organs under it in a dark red blur of blood and flesh. 'Twas the still soft breast, still round and white with thin veins of blue accenting the tenderness and fineness of her, like a China porcelain so delicate it was transparent, his very first sight of female nakedness, that had caused Miles Hawkes to marvel how anyone could cast such beauty down.

"Oh, Eli! 'Tis wrong to look upon 'er, I'm sure!"

One of the women proclaimed, wiping her nose and eyes from crying.

"Aye, that," Eli agreed and, as he knelt, began moving the sand back over her. "May God 'ave mercy on 'er soul."

"Amen." replied the others.

Only Elizabeth Treadwell and Rosie Low had been silent. Tom Treadwell and Ned Low had not come home that night. Not to Rosie's, nor to Elizabeth's. The two women gazed as though through the woman into the earth and far beyond to the dark nothingness of the grave. Their fear was mixed with a dull hope, for the boys had done this before and come home next day, laughing, feigning shame, in too good spirits to be daunted by discipline, especially if their fathers were from home. And Rosie, at least, like many mothers of sons, so glad to see them strong and brave, had not scolded hers and let him laugh.

Let him laugh. If only she could let him laugh now, Rosie mused, all t'would be well an' fine. If only she had let him laugh, thought Elizabeth, what she would give now.

'Twas then, the young Daniel Pritchard ran down on the beach, having spotted something strange from his window.

Daniel shouted to the group. "There be a long stick poking up through the rocks! What is it?"

What could it be? All turned their attention to him.

"Where is this stick, Daniel?"

"There!"

All turned to see exactly that, a stick, yanked this way and that by the surf.

They set off together, but it was Rosie who got there first. In time to see a large, black boot thrust crazily out from the rocks, a thick leg, a fearsome, bloated black body bobbing up and down on the waves, floating Indie scarves and blouse blown up with water, anger 'pon his fierce face, fury, more like, his stubby hands swelled up with water, rising and falling with the swells and from his chest, from a swollen red wound, straight up with all the passion from which it had been thrown, a child's toy, though a real weapon in every way. The carved initials, NL, swayed back and forth on the spear's end.

"Ned! Oh, my Ned! My Ned!" Rosie screamed to the ocean and to the sky. She turned then and screamed also to the land, as if not knowing which way to run to look for him.

"Oh, Ned," she sank to her knees. She covered her face with her hands. Not even prayer could help, she knew, in her soul.

Then, Elizabeth saw something red caught on the pirate's Spanish boot, a thread of wool, flaming in the cool, blue surf. She reached, and out from under this hulking body, she pulled what seemed familiar, and was. A scarlet ball of yarn, dripping with salt water.

Rosie uncovered her eyes just in time to see it, before Elizabeth could thrust it under her clothes. 'Twas Molly's ball of yarn, Rosie saw instantly, that she'd tossed earlier that day, how long ago and where?

He'd taken it! Her Ned had taken the girl's charm!

Then, Rosie let out a shriek from so far down, willingly, she would give forth all the life she held within her.

In the turmoil, Tom Treadwell, as though risen from the grave, stood and stumbled toward them. Elizabeth saw him, as though in a dream, was he really there? Yes. And, no. He was alive, but not the same Tom, for he would walk, ever with a falter, and not for many years would he speak a word.

Marblehead, 1991

Chapter 22

The storm had put on quite a show.

They named it Hurricane Bob. Bob Simmons got kidded a lot. People asked, "What About Bob?" after the movie, over and over, like no one had ever heard it before.

All over town, through out the night, electrical boxes exploded like bombs, one after another, louder than the thunder and lightning, unfathomable booms that woke people and started small fires. The rain was torrential; it sliced sideways in vast sheets, cutting through the shrieking wind from sky to earth.

A street sign was found stuck like an axe in a chimney. Cars flipped over in driveways. Boats sailed the sky and moored in treetops. Some trees bent their heads to the ground. Others reappeared surrealistically where they should not have been: poking out of the windows of houses and cars, lying across the road, growing out of a flatbed truck.

All the flowers in Marblehead were killed by the beating they took from the storm and by the surprise of salt that settled on them: they gathered in sopping piles that backed up the gutters, they turned the landscape of the shore black and brittle.

Peter didn't care about the storm. He'd evacuated the children early on. Brought them to their grandmother's in Salem where he sat in the living room and watched the hurricane on TV. His beard was three weeks old; he forgot to eat, to wash, to sleep, though he'd pass out now and then and wake sweating in terror that he was suffocating under something he couldn't lift and when he tried to scream, his mouth opened, but no sound came out. He hated waking from that nightmare. There are nightmares you wake from, he'd think, and nightmares you wake into.

When he went home, finally, things looked right. He opened the delicate French doors Beth had put in to overlook the ocean; they were unbroken and still standing, though most of the wall was gone. Peter laughed a little and whimpered too, as he entered what was once their home. He sat down in his recliner, in the puddle that had formed in its seat, and faced what used to be the television.

A gigantic boulder had smashed down where the television once stood. Must have weighed eight hundred pounds, come through the roof.

Peter broke down then and sobbed, crying for the first time since they had taken Bethie out of the sea and put her into the ground. He sobbed deeper than he thought possible, harder than he knew was healthy. He felt his guts coming up and he didn't care. He vomited into his lap and just sat there, looking at the pile of his own slime. He laughed. He laughed, at himself and at this leviathan he'd inherited, grey as an elephant, big as a dinosaur, fallen, like a message from God.

It seemed so right.

Marblehead, 1991

Chapter 23

Cassandra Diamond Hawkes was at Kristin Feingold's house for a meeting about diversity in town real estate. She wasn't sure what the whole thing was about, but she thought it was about getting more diverse ethnic groups to buy real estate. Of course, if they were buying, they'd be rich ethnics, so that was okay. Money was green.

Cassandra was studying to get her real estate license. It was a chance to be financially independent, and she had to try it, though she found it hard to retain a lot of the information, most of which seemed irrelevant to her - it couldn't be *that* complicated to find someone a house - she just kept trying to make sense of it. She had to get this right, she told herself; she had to try to make a decent living. She had been invited this evening, she assumed, because she knew so much about the town's history. Kristen had asked her to speak to the group about the Native Americans and African Americans who used to live amongst the townspeople. That was 300 years ago, and most of them were slaves or servants, Cassandra had told her, but, no matter, Kristen had insisted.

She felt uncomfortable. Everyone was so well dressed, so wealthy. Why, the watch on Kristin Feingold's wrist alone would pay her rent for a year. The diamond rings on Kristin's pudgy fingers could sail her round the world and back. It made her shudder, fearfully, at the order of things.

What were they talking about? Something was sending stabs of anxiety through her belly. Kristin was speaking to the group.

"We're so glad that Frankie got off with second degree murder. Manslaughter would have been better, but God knows, second degree is better than first any day of the week! At least he has a chance of parole. Okay! Well, on to the next order of business. Cassandra Diamond Hawkes! Our own little sculptor will say a few words about the town's history of diversity, as well as her new career in real estate and how she came to support diversity in town realty. Cass?"

No one ever called her Cass. Only Mrs. Treadwell, Beth, had. Town realty. How could she support town realty when she had no realty? *She got an image then, of her old house, floating out to sea.*

Cassandra got up, as she knew she was supposed to, and traveled blindly to the middle of the room. There, she faced the group. About thirty townspeople in local government and commerce. Something was happening again, she knew, for she'd lost her eyesight. She staggered. Soon, she comforted herself, her inner eye would open. Sure enough, *the whoosh came down in a wedge, this time of crystal blue light and Kristin's colonial living room split right down the middle leaving Cassandra rocking precariously on the deck of the*

Rosebud. She steadied her sea legs. She wasn't blind any more. She saw the ocean, greenish and choppy, the Cal losing its grip on the waves. Dancing crazily. No one was at the helm.

Cassandra's head hurt, the back of her skull, on the right. She touched her hand there and the fingers came away bloody. That might not be real. She saw the pretty blonde head patched with blood. Cassandra seemed to turn to the group, but in her reality sleep, she saw Beth fall. Blood on the deck, blood on the sails! A sudden terror of what she had done overcame her, of what had been done, she, Cassandra, was not there, she told herself, her mouth opened as if to say so, but his voice came out!

Sh-sh-sh-sh-she-she-she screeeeemed! Sh-sh-shee, why'd she havta dooo that? She scared me! She didn' have to sc-scream like that! Why'd sh-she havta do that? Hur' my ears, scared me so much. Cassandra swooned, almost passed out, to feel him squirming inside her.

Then, Cassandra whispered, as if in confidence to the group, a real scream scares you more than the movies! If you heard her, if you, I hope no one heard her, it was so scary. They'd be scared.

I 'm not gonna hur-hurt ya, I not gonna, it doesn' havta hurt, it's mos' natr'l thing in the worl', in the worl', I'll take ya' round the worl', we could get married in Cancun, Jamaica, d'ya make ha'? I wanna take care of you forever. I love makin' love to you; I've always loved you, Beth! Beth!

Pretty little Bethie! My pretty white bird. Mmmm, Cassandra *moaned.*

No! No! A trickle of blood is sliding back and forth along the deck of the Rosebud, sliding, my own, or his or both, what's that sound, hollow, metal, the spinnaker pole sliding back and forth, slams against the cabin, hollow screams, slams against my legs, don't hit me, lift my head, can't lift my head, he's heavy, can't breathe, ugh, only Peter's been inside me, oh, God, no, no, get off of me, get off of me!

I won' leave you, I'll nevva leave you, I'd havta be nuts, whaddya think, that I'd leave ya, like in white slav'ry or somethin', ha, ha, ha, she's stronger than I thought! All that flyin' round like a white bird! Her w-wi-wings stronger than I thought. She fights me! Stop it, stop fighting me, it's me, me! You like me! You're supposed to like me! It's the clothes! We should sail naked, perflecly nat'ral. Sail naked. Like we were meant to sail, it means so much to me.

She tasted like the sea, warm like the sun.

Cassandra looked down at the Oriental rug on the floor, *but she saw not a rug, or a floor, but the fiberglass deck of a sailboat, on which a golden body, a sun-browned body of a woman, her sunny hair fanning out around her frightened face. Beth's face, bewildered, horrified.*

From the antique sea chest that served as a coffee table, without knowing what she did, Cassandra picked up a brass telescope. Raising this above her head, Cassandra grimaced as in fury and sent her weapon down, swinging it just above a certain spot on the rug. The group gasped in unison as Cassandra beat the woman's invisible body about the head and neck, the group saw nothing, but to Cassandra's eyes, *Beth's body jerked up and down with each blow, over and over Cassandra hit her, screaming as she did,*

What were you thinking? I never wan'ned to hurt you! Are you crazy or something? Are you crazy? Huh? Huh? Huh? Huh?

Hurts, oh, God, what, why, God, it hurts, Em, Emily, your little face, Peter, Pete, forgive me, eyes roll, my eyes, white cloud, shining with sun, oh, God, is it You? For this shining cloud, I thank you, God.

Answer me! Answer me! Oh, no, now she's not answering me!

Is she dead? Oh, Je-sus! Now, whad'she havta do that for? Jesus, now no one'll believe me, now I'm dead, she isn't dead, she can't be dead, she can't be. Doesn' seem real; her head flops so stupidly when I pick it up, whaddya stupid now? Ya gotcha self all bloody, bloody, oh, Jeez, gotta clean up, gotta clean that up, towels, I can use the sea, looka the people on shore, they're ants! Ants! Scurry, scurry, go get some money! Gotta get rid of this, this thing! Weigh her down, weigh her down deep, the deep, the deep, where is it deep enough? Where am I now?

The sun is blinding me, blinding, where is it deep enough, dark enough, deep enough?

Did anyone hear her scream? Cassandra asked the group.

The good citizens in the room stared at her in amazement, unsure whether they'd seen a play, a monologue or had just witnessed this bizarre woman go completely mad.

Marblehead, 1991

Chapter 24

On the day Beth Treadwell went sailing with Frank Girelli, Mrs. Lena Symonds had just finished washing up the medicine glass from the afternoon. This she carefully refilled with water, set on a nice tray with the measured dose next to it, ready to be mixed. She liked things to be nice, even unpleasant things. No reason at all for the medicines to be offensive. After all, they gave comfort, didn't they? Lena was proud of her work. She considered herself a comfort to her patient, old Mrs. Gatchell, Ruth, who'd had a stroke last year and was unable to help herself, poor dear.

Lena sighed and adjusted her pesky uniform which was slightly too snug for her around the waist and kept catching uncomfortably, causing her to itch in a maddening way -

Suddenly, the most gruesome shriek she'd ever heard in her entire life came piercing through her ears, tearing into her brain.

Immediately, she looked out the picture window, which faced the ocean on the seaward side of the Neck. The sea was a lovely aqua; white tipped waves lapped playfully against the rocky shore of the small island out there. She saw no boat, no yacht, no sign of activity. Nothing but blue ocean and blue sky.

She listened, careful not to make a sound. She held her breath. Her heart throbbed in her chest, her head actually hurt with the tension of listening. The silence was so complete; Lena became overwhelmed with - loneliness - that surely didn't come from her. She was never lonely. She had too much to do with Ruth and her own family. It was a pure loneliness that had come from that voice. Or, the absence of that voice. Whew, Lena shrugged her shoulders as if to shrug off the feeling - the willies, she called it.

Still, Lena was disturbed. She was absolutely positive she'd heard a woman scream. And - not in fun, no, not in fun. No, and not like the movies at all. No actress could duplicate that horrible sound. She could still - well, feel it, inside her own chest, filling her with the most unbelievable fear and sorrow and regret and - more than that, terror! And, disbelief, and, anguish, oh, where were all these feelings coming from?

Should she report it? And say what? That she'd heard a woman scream, when? Let's see, couldn't have been more than five minutes ago. Four thirty-five. Maybe, she'd call. She had so much to do. Maybe, in a minute.

Lena opened the dryer door, checked the clothes, all done. Methodically, slowly as was her manner, she began folding. She *could* call while she folded. Hmm. Would she seem like a kook? Then, suddenly, she recalled that story, that old Marblehead tale the teacher used to tell when Lena was in school of a Screeching Woman. Oh, Lord, that woman who was murdered by pirates in Lovis Cove three hundred years ago and they say you can still hear her scream. Gee whiz, good thing she thought of that! The police would've laughed at her.

My, my.

Still. Lena was upset. Her usual complacency had been disrupted in the most disquieting way. Some violence had occurred, somewhere. In her heart, she knew she'd heard a woman scream. Nothing could erase that knowledge.

But, which woman had she actually heard? Someone out there now or - oh, no, what if she had heard the woman of the legend?

Oh, that would be too strange! Lena laughed out loud, and then, was pulled back to an eerie sadness by that same nagging feeling of horror that lingered in her heart but was not her own.

Epilogue

Marblehead, 1993

It was a picture postcard day, cloudless and warm.

After the ceremony of candles and prayers and wreathes of flowers floating in the surf, which had been beautiful and meant to cleanse the island and the ocean around it of the violation which had occurred there, Cassandra stood admiring the long-stemmed cosmos and delicate white gaura of the garden they had made together nodding and dancing in the breeze.

Julie Low Peach and Bill Peach were present, as was Jo Pritchard. Peter Treadwell, looking exhausted and shipwrecked, held the two-year-old Emily in his arms. All the children were dressed up and, including the youngest, solemnly, eerily, quiet.

Bob Simmons and Julie's husband, Bill, had prepared the soil for Beth's memorial garden, which had been ceremoniously planted there by the group days earlier. She, Cassandra, had been proud to plant a small rose bush, miniature white roses, which were so like Mrs. Treadwell, Beth, she waited till no one was looking and kissed what she thought were the tender cheeks of their white petals.

Beth's best friend had placed the tall grasses in the earth. "You have your garden of grasses, Bethie," Julie had said, tearfully, "that will sing for you forever."

Julie broke down then, remembering only vaguely in her sorrow, that Beth had wanted the memorial garden for a slave, a child, and this fact just broke her heart all over again.

Jo Pritchard had planted ivy for eternity. Bob Simmons stayed as close to her as possible. They'd been on two dates already, and Bob was hopeful. Jo was different since Beth's murder, quieter, more thoughtful. She seemed to lean on him every time they were together. He wanted her to lean on him, and then get stronger. He wanted to help her do that.

Beth's husband, Peter, on his knees, had been the one to tuck in the forget-me-nots that Beth had loved; tiny, blue and seemingly, insignificant. Each of the children had buried a bulb for next spring, as it was almost the time for autumn bulbs, almost, not quite, but no one was concerned. And, that seemed right to Cassandra. Nothing could die that Beth would be taking care of.

The group stood for a long time in silence. The white boats sailed, the gulls sang out with joy as they glided on full wing. The sea washed rhythmically ashore, the sky gazed inscrutably blue and the flowers began the process of sending their roots down and their faces up.

Marblehead, 1695

Tom Treadwell was leaning on the hoe, gazing dreamily at nothing. He was older, paler, and weaker.

A family of fat rabbits hopped down the trail by the garden. Almost at once, they began nibbling on the new grass.

Leaning on the hoe, Tom stared at the rabbits. He could see their tiny hearts beating rapidly under their fur.

Emily suddenly burst out of the house. She, too, was older, a robust child of five years.

Emily ran to Tom. Gently, she took the hoe from his limp hand.

"Here's how to weed, Thomas!" Emily cried out eagerly as she turned the hoe, much larger than herself, like an expert gardener. "I will show you! Look! Watch me!"

But, Tom did not turn his head to see what his sister was doing. With tear-filled eyes, he watched the family of rabbits peacefully eating.

About the Author

Patricia Goodwin grew up in an Italian-American neighborhood outside of Boston. She was the first in her family to finish high school and go on to college. She graduated cum laude from Salem State University, Salem, MA where she earned a BA in English Literature.

In the early days of the natural foods movement, she created and taught macrobiotic educational programs for the East West Foundation, Brookline, MA (now the Kushi Institute, Becket, MA). She has practiced the macrobiotic discipline since 1974.

Patricia has written many articles of non-fiction, which have appeared in publications such as *The Boston Herald, The Record American, American Express OnTime, AAA Horizons, The Marblehead Reporter* and *The North Shore Sunday*.

"A Child's Christmas in Revere", a chapter from her novel, *Holy Days* was published in the anthology, *Under Her Skin: How Girls Experience Race in America* (Seal Press, 2004). Her poetry has been published in *Marblehead Magazine, IndeArts, Runes, nthposition.com, Pemmican Press,* and *Radius: Poetry from the Center to the Edge*, among others. In 2012, her poem "the last day" will be published in *The Potomac*. She has three books of poetry: *Marblehead Moon* (Plum Press, 1993), *Java Love* (Plum Press, 1997), and *Atlantis* (Plum Press, 2006).

Patricia lives with her husband and daughter in an historic seacoast town in Massachusetts.

For more information about the author, including new work, events, and videos, please visit patriciagoodwin.com.